FICTION HOUSE PRESS
PRESENTS

SPICY STORIES

March 1938
Vol. VIII, No. 3

This reprint edition is a facsimile of the original pulp magazine. Variations in printing and quality can be attributed to the original magazine which was printed on rough woodpulp paper.

ISBN 978-1-64720-105-0

www.FictionHousePress.com
fictionhousepress@gmail.com

American Medical Opinion—"A practical work written in plain, **understandable** language with a modern point of view. The author has **certainly** been guided by good judgment as to what constitutes general medical opinion."—**Journal of the American Medical Association**

because--

—they did not know the **latest facts** about sex revealed in this amazing book. They relied on instinct—**and instinct led them astray. He did not know** the science of perfect mating. **He did not know** the secrets of "love play." **She did not know** what to allow a lover to do. She confused ignorance with innocence. THEY BOTH BUNGLED and paid the terrible price which Nature extorts from those who THINK they know but don't!

Tells What to Do and How

What to Do Before, During and After Sexual Intercourse. By means of EXPLANATORY DIAGRAMS and clearly written directions Dr. Hutton shows HOW to arouse the "sexually slow" wife, **how to avoid hurting the nervous system**, tells how FREQUENTLY sexual intercourse should take place, describes the six different positions for sexual intercourse **and when to use them.**

Using plain language, this book gives such definite and detailed information regarding the sex act that no married couple need any longer remain in ignorance of **exactly how it should be performed.** It is a book for **husband and wife to read together.**

Subjects Embraced

Preparation for Marriage . . . Sex Instinct in Men; in Women . . . The Technique of the Sex-Act . . . Practical Considerations . . . The First Sex Act . . . Adjustment to Sex Life; Difficulties; **Mutual** Consideration . . . Frequency of Intercourse . . . Variety in Performing the Sex-Act . . . Influence of Age, Sex Instinct, Health . . . Sex Intercourse during Pregnancy; After Childbirth . . . Inability to Perform Sexually . . . Menstruation and the "Change of Life" . . . Curable Childlessness . . . The Value of Birth Control.

FIVE EXPLANATORY DIAGRAMS

Reveals Long-Hidden Secrets!

No matter how long you are married you NEED this book NOW! Its new and remarkable revelations will astonish you—yet they are scientific and reliable. It will teach you things you never knew before—some only recently discovered—and show you how to regain the marriage joys you thought were lost and share happily the spiritual as well as the physical intimacies of the COMPLETE sex life!

Nothing essential is omitted or left in any obscurity. The book came to be written because Dr. Hutton saw the terrible tragedies, the nervous breakdowns, the blighted bodies, the domestic discords, the children made miserable because of sexual ignorance—and saw the crying **need for sound, simple, practical, definite and detailed information about sex behavior in marriage!**

Why follow old-fashioned methods which modern medical science has discarded? Why indulge in health-destroying habits and customs which have been found to be entirely wrong?

Why remain in ignorance another day? Enjoy the happiness this book has brought to thousands of joyfully married couples. Return the coupon at once. This book will come to you in plain wrapper on our FREE trial offer!

READ FIRST THEN DECIDE!
SEND NO MONEY

These Questions That Blast Many Marriages—Answered Fearlessly and Frankly!

WHO is to blame for "sexual frigidity?" How can **impotence** be overcome? **Honeymoon tragedies**—how to avoid them! Is intercourse advisable during pregnancy? What is the TRUTH about Birth Control? Why is **sex-starvation** harmful to married people? How to solve the problem of the **"undersexed"** or **"oversexed"**? What must one do to achieve **sexual satisfaction** in marriage? What should husband and wife know about each other's organs of sex? What is the effect of **sexual experimentation** on married life?

And Many Other Vital Questions

Mail This Coupon NOW

HEALTHCRAFT, INC., Dept. 369-A,
247 West 19th St., New York City.

Send me "Sex Technique in Marriage" in plain wrapper marked "Personal". I will pay $1.98 and few cents postage on delivery. I MUST BE SATISFIED or I will return book within 5 days and you will refund purchase price. (I am over 21 years old.)

Name . . . .

Address . . . .

☐ CHECK HERE if you wish to enclose only $1.98 with coupon, thus saving delivery charges. **(Same money-back guarantee.)**

MARCH
1938
VOLUME VIII
NUMBER 3

SPARKLING FEATURES

PEPPY STORIES

SPICY STORIES is published monthly by the
D. M. Publishing Co., Inc., Dover, Del.

The publishers are not responsible for the return of unsolicited manuscripts.

Between You And Me!

NOTICE:—No letter will be published unless the writer gives permission to print his or her full name and address.—*The Editor.*

Dear Editor:

Just a couple of rooters rooting for "Spicy". Swell idea of yours to put in so many joke pages and cartoons; they're always good and very amusing; the pictures are getting more and more attractive, and we can't think of a better way to get rid of two bits every month than to buy "Spicy", turn the lights down low, have the best bottle of Scotch on the floor very near, the tallest glasses in the house filled to the top, arms around each other, and reading the pages of "Spicy" together from start to finish! Some set-up, eh? Well, that's what we do every month, and take it from us, it's better than any last row of any movie theatre! Our motto is, "Stick to Home and Spicy!" It works every time.

Teeny and Bill Watkins
Buffalo, New York

Dear Editor:

I have been a reader of your periodical "Spicy Stories" for a long time and I consider it one of the greatest of its kind on the market today. I especially enjoy your "Between You And Me" department and consider it one of your greatest features. I shall look forward to the publication of this letter in an early issue as I am very much in need of pen pals. Behind my loneliness there is a great story which I shall relate to my pals who answer this letter. I have been considered very handsome but hope you will forgive me for saying so—I will let you decide that after you see my picture which I promise to send you if you write. I am 26 years old, have dark wavy brown hair, blue eyes, weigh 150 lbs., 5 ft. 8 in. tall, have traveled extensively throughout all 48 of these U.S.A., Canada, Mexico. I've been writing songs in Hollywood since 1930 and will send a complimentary copy of one of same (personally autographed) to you if you write. Believe it or not. Won't you all write, please?

Your Pal,
Irving Siegel
3638 *Dwiggins St., Los Angeles, California*

Dear Editor:

The "Between You And Me" feature of your very excellent magazine is just about the best thing and I've finally decided to join it. "Spicy" has long been a favorite of mine and I wouldn't miss an issue of it. Last year I went to Palestine and spent six months there; I met lots of interesting people and made many friends, but my Old Stand-by, Old Reliable, and Old Trusty, "Spicy" was always with me, as I had ordered it sent to me from the States.

While in that strange fascinating country I introduced "Spicy" to my new friends and they all became strong boosters for it. I still correspond with many of them, and as soon as I've finished with my latest copy, I ship it right out to them. Our letters are often filled with exchanges of ideas and opinions about the swell stories in the magazine. Most of us agree that the one who writes the best ones is Phyllis Hoerner, and second is Tom Kane.

I didn't intend to make this such a long letter, but when I get started raving about "Spicy" I guess my enthusiasm runs away with me. I just thought you'd like to know that your magazine has ardent fans in other places outside of this country. I hope it continues to be printed forever.

Molly Madison
Bangor, Maine

... Try, Try Again!

By

PATSY HUNT

She had come upon them snuggled in a corner, arms wound around each other.

IT WAS a darned good thing the Jennings' house was enormous. Almost a week before the third of February, which was the day Marjorie Jennings was to make her debut, numerous friends from the city began to arrive and the Jennings started paying the penalty of living in the country. By the second, the congestion was so bad that it was almost impossible to walk through the drawing room without interrupting a dozen couples in the throes of love and equally as many approaching it with sighs and *oh's* and *ah's*.

As for the stairway and hidden nooks and corners, young men and women fought valiantly for such seclusion. There was continuous drinking in the dining room, breakfast room ,music room and library. It was whoopla from morning until morning, interrupted only at short intervals for sleep and eats and the change of clothes.

It was all perfectly hectic. Mrs. Jennings bore up nobly for a week then she took to her bed in the isolation of her own room. Being a chaperone to her daughter's friends was well and good if one was an octopus. But she wasn't an octopus and she didn't have eyes fore and aft and she no sooner stopped one couple from flinging too much woo than another enamoured pair caught her attention. She lost three pounds leaping about in the course of her duties; her lovely silver-gray hair changed imperceptibly to white and her blue eyes became hollow.

"Nature," Mrs. Jennings finally consoled herself from the depths of her satin sheets, "will simply have to take its course! What else can you expect when girls go unbrassiered, ungirdled and practically undressed! I give up! I wash my hands of everything!"

And she thought all over again what a silly formality it was for a girl now days to make a debut; especially her own daughter. Marjorie had actually been "out" since she was fourteen. And at nineteen, judging from the conduct of her intimates, there certainly wasn't anything a doting mother could tell her! She thought a little of her own youth and a long gone time when a girl really "came out" at her debut.

Marjorie, of course, would have all the trappings and the trimmings of an innocent. She would be surrounded by flowers; she would stand and receive her guests in the traditional virginal white; her blue eyes would be starry and tremulous and her golden hair would shine like a halo above goodness knows what sort of wild thoughts! And when she finally took Marjorie off to tell her of the ways of the world and the perfidy of men it would probably end up by Marjorie opening her mother's eyes to a thing or two!

"The whole business is a farce from beginning to end! I wonder why we modern mothers keep it up!" groaned Mrs. Jennings and tried not to hear the surreptitious feet that were slipping past her door to the privacy of the sitting rooms along the hall.

MARJORIE AT THE MOMENT was having her own problen. She was lying across a chaise-longue in a wisp of blue satin panties and a blue thread of lace across the bulging beauty of her own breasts. She was thinking of Daisy Quentin and that her mother had had the nerve inviting Daisy to assist at the debut, even if Daisy's mother and Mrs. Jennings had been friends for thirty years.

For Daisy and Marjorie weren't friends and never would be. In the first place, they looked a little bit alike. They were both honey blondes, slender and rather small, with luscious milky-white bosoms and shoulders. They both had perfect slim legs, narrow waists and rather heavy hips which swayed a little when they walked. Just that resemblance was sufficient in itself to cause a deep, instinctive dislike between any two females. But this slight similarity in looks wasn't the only reason for Marjorie's dislike of Daisy Quentin.

It seemed to Marjorie that whenever Daisy was around, unpleasant things began to happen. If Marjorie saw a man she wanted Daisy was after him like a sick kitten for a hot brick—and vice versa. Usually Daisy got the man. Daisy had a way of dancing sensuously close, her firm feminine rondures mashed against her victim's bosom; Daisy had a way of leaning over tables so that the deep V of her scanty bodice showed startlingly inviting glimpses. Daisy had a way of looking into a man's eyes and promising him ecstasy with a single look; and Daisy, Marjorie knew full well, drew the line at little.

MARJORIE HAD A TECHNIQUE, too. She knew when and just how much of a silken leg to expose; her eyes could promise heavens knows how much. She was entirely familiar as to how a gaping V could attract masculine notice. But the trouble was that Daisy was quick, an art she had learned by being some three years older than Marjorie. And by the time Marjorie got her stuff under way the object of the conquest was always under Daisy's spell. He usually didn't come to until both she and Marjorie had set their gazes upon some other unsuspecting male. And Marjorie, of course, wasn't going to take on any girl's left-over!

This very thing had happened last night. A slim, tall, blond young man had arrived at the house from Hartford. He was Henry Dyke, a friend of the family's, and enormously good looking. She and Daisy, standing by the mantel, sipping cocktails and making nasty passes at each other, had seen him come in. Marjorie had watched Daisy's big bosom begin to heave with a tell-tale interest.

She had looked down upon her own luscious figure and had been shocked at its tremulous movements. In a sort of daze Marjorie had watched Daisy put down her cocktail glass, wriggle her hips a little and smooth down her silken bodice. She had watched a certain light come into Daisy's blue eyes and she had told herself, feverishly, "Damn it, Daisy won't get ahead of me this time!"

But Daisy had. Almost before Marjorie had gotten herself collected Daisy was hanging on the young man's arm. And a little later, wandering about the big house looking for him, she had come upon Daisy and Henry snuggled back in a corner, their arms wound around each other and their lips warmly clinging. She had stood there looking at the man's slim, caressing fingers, at the white gleam of Daisy's undraped shoulder and had wondered, passionately, how she could get even with Daisy Quentin.

Marjorie's fist sent him down with a thud!

SHE WAS STILL wondering at dinner. They had reached the dessert course when Marjorie noticed Daisy leaning close to Babs Lee and whispering solemnly:

"You're positive John Smith will get here, Babs? Because really it was the prospect of his coming that made me accept Mrs. Jennings' invitation to assist at Marjorie's debut. You know, of course, that Marjorie and I can't endure each other!"

Babs said, "So that's why you're here? I had wondered. Well, ease your pain, my love. John's coming. He was too busy at the office to get away for the preliminary festivities but he'll be here for the debut. He told me so. He'll arrive on the 10:10 train in the morning."

"It was cheeky of me to invite him when Marjorie and Mrs. Jennings don't even know him. But I wanted to see him again and this seemed a swell unobvious way to bring it about. I've been cherishing his memory ever since you introduced me to him last June. Frankly, Babs, the man knocked me for a loop!"

"Don't they all," said Babs, a little sourly.

Daisy grinned brightly. "No, darling," she answered, softly. "Not the way John Smith did. The others were mere flurries—he was the works. You know, I always did like tall, lean, dark men. And when tall, lean, dark men . . ." Daisy bent closer to Babs, lowering her voice even below a whisper.

But not low enough for Marjorie to miss what she was saying. Marjorie sat there with her heart pounding. It was almost indecent the way Daisy was describing everything about John Smith. No man likes his amorous tactics dangled about for the delectation of a disinterested party. Why if John Smith could hear Daisy now he'd turn red, white and blue behind the ears.

"And when that man finally kissed me," Daisy was finishing excitedly, "you can bet I was awfully thrilled!"

Marjorie had snorted to herself. Daisy was the biggest damned fool, she had thought coldly. She had hoped fervently that Daisy would trip over her trailing flounces when she was pushing cookies at the debut and break her legs. It would, reflected Marjorie with mild detachment, serve her right. But if Daisy did she would probably take advantage of the accident to let her shoulder straps fall down her arms or her skirt billow up about her lovely white thighs. Daisy was like that. If Daisy fell down a well she'd come up with two good looking guys, one on each arm!

MARJORIE THOUGHT, SUDDENLY thankful, "Jimmy will be in after dinner. There's one man Daisy can't make!" For Jimmy Diggs belonged to Marjorie. All summer they had spent the long, idle days together. They had clung to each other in secluded wooded spots. They had ridden horseback into the mountains and had flung themselves on beds of violets and had been wrapped in each other's arms for long, golden hours. Marjorie didn't particularly care for Jimmy. He was short and redheaded and quite an old shoe. Old shoes gave a girl a pinch now and then but they didn't keep her interested. But Jimmy was perfectly swell when a girl was feeling a bit romantic and in a receptive mood.

"Good old, Jimmy," Marjorie had thought on, "at least I can depend on him."

Jimmy had arrived promptly after dinner. Jimmy was like that—you could depend on him. Or so Marjorie had thought all summer. But she was to discover, before the end of that bitter evening, that a girl could depend on nothing, on no one; least of all a man—any man. In no time at all Jimmy's mouth was gaping over Dasy, Jimmy's eyes were clinging to those luscious rondures just as if Marjorie was some flat-chested dame who wore goggles. And finally Jimmy and Daisy hid themselves in the library.

Marjorie, tipping quietly down the hall in the dark, had thrust her head inside. And there, with the moonlight slanting across them, she had seen the man she trusted and the girl she despised, all wound up together like a one cent pretzel. "You'd think she could wait for her John Smith," Marjorie had groaned, sickly. "But maybe Daisy goes on the theme that practice makes perfect or something!"

ALL LAST NIGHT Marjorie had hated Daisy with an intense, searing hatred. She hated Jimmy, too, when she stopped to think about him. But *Daisy*—first the tall, blond Henry Dyke and then Jimmy. It was too much. Human nature rebels at some things; even the staunchest character can stand just so much, and then it begins to warp or ache to strike back.

Marjorie's was a strike back character. Lying on the chaise-longue with her debut tea only a few hours off, her thoughts were anything but those of a sweet young thing who is about to be launched on the social world. "If only I could take her John Smith away from her," thought Marjorie, hotly. "If only I could rush right into him before she gets her greedy claws into him! If only I could sweep him off his feet and give Daisy a potent dose of her own medicine!"

If she could do this, Marjorie knew, she would certainly have done *something!* For before, Daisy had only annexed men that she, Marjorie had coveted but not loved. And Daisy loved John Smith. John Smith was the first and only man who had ever actually knocked Daisy for a loop. John Smith was the means by which Marjorie could get her revenge.

Suddenly Marjorie jerked upright on the chaise, her big bosom bobbing up and down, her blue eyes glued on the Dresden mantel clock. It was only eight-fifteen. There was plenty of time before the 10:10 train! With that thought Marjorie sailed out into the hall, her feather trimmed mules beating out a staccato on the polished floor and her breasts matching the rhythm.

She stuck her head in the parlor maid's door and said, breathlessly, "Colleen, I forgot to tell you that Miss Quentin doesn't wish to be awakened this morning. Not until noon. And, Colleen, have Jibbs bring around the station wagon for me. I'm going to meet Miss Quentin's guest for her!"

Ducking back into her room Marjorie ran smack-dab into Henry Dyke. Henry was all attention now. His blue eyes ran over Marjorie quickly, warmly. He put a detaining hand on Marjorie's bare shoulder. He said, "Say-y, where have *you* been hiding!" and would have drawn her into his arms. But Marjorie swung out a fist, clipped him on the chin and he went down with a thud. "Daisy's left-over!" snapped Marjorie and darted into her room.

THREE MEN ALIGHTED from the 10:10 train One was tall and pale and rather sickly looking; one was short and fat with a little paunch of a stomach swollen out in front of him. Both of these men stared at Marjorie with eyes that moved from the crown of her golden head to the tips of her patent toes and then back to the luscious pout of her breasts. Both of them licked their lips appreciatively, particularly the tall, pale, sickish chap. Indeed, the tall one made a move toward Marjorie, his eyes light and watery on her clinging blue silk dress—a queer sort of gaze, it was, that made Marjorie feel slightly naked.

But it was the third man that finally caught and held Marjorie's attention. He was tall and dark and ridiculously handsome. He was, Marjorie knew instantly, Daisy's John Smith. She would have known him anywhere. He was precisely the sort of man who could knock Daisy for a loop. He was young and tweedy and his dark hair was indubitably curly. He was excitingly virile with a high color, broad muscle-packed shoulders and incredibly long legs. He stood there on the platform, gazing about rather uncertainly, as though looking for some one. That someone, of course, was Daisy who was unsuspectingly sleeping through all this intrigue.

"Hello, John Smith," said Marjorie gayly. She didn't go toward him. She achieved her best effects, she knew, from standing at a little distance where he could take in the whole flowing effect of her snug blue silk dress, the deep V that slashed down between her mature breasts and accentuated their jutting splendor, and the short skirt that was perhaps a trifle too short but effective.

The young man smiled. A little whistle of awed admiration came through his lips.

"Everybody at the house is asleep so I've been delegated to come in the station wagon and drag you back to the festivities. Your date had a big night and was clean tuckered out as we say up in these parts. I hope—you don't mind."

"Mind?" John Smith's dark eyes moved slowly over Marjorie. They were keen, young

She came awake then, her young body meeting pressure with pressure, kiss with kiss.

eyes. They didn't miss a thing. For a moment those eyes clung to the V which remained discreetly closed when she held her breath and yet opened just wide enough when she spoke to reveal the beginning of firmly modeled white mounds. "I'm sure," he said at last, moving his gaze from those luscious juts to her eyes, "that I don't mind at all."

"Not disappointed?"

"Heavens—no!" said John Smith. "In fact, I'm elated. I'm out of my solemn head with joy!"

IT WAS A LINE, of course. Daisy had whispered last night at dinner what a line the man had. Daisy had whispered other things to Babs about John Smith and suddenly remembering them made Marjorie's heart leap and her legs go weak beneath her. She found herself looking at John Smith's mouth and wondering how it would feel on her own; she found herself gazing at his hands, remembering what Daisy had said about those hands and how they could caress; she found herself looking at the whole powerful virility of him. And she colored faintly in spite of herself.

"I knew I was of an emotional nature," she thought clearly. "But I mustn't mix pleasure with business. My business is to get even with Daisy. Keep your head, woman! Don't go gaga and spoil everything now!"

But in the station wagon, riding through the beautiful crisply cold day, her little mink cape close about her throat, Marjorie found it almost impossible to concentrate on Daisy. She was too terribly conscious of the young man beside her. She hadn't counted on him affecting her like this. She hadn't expected her heart to go leaping and bounding about and her knees to tremble. She could feel his dark eyes on her. And out of the tail of her own she was watching his fingers. Those same fingers came out as if to close over her own on the steering wheel.

No matter how crazy he was about Daisy and Daisy about him, the thing had gone so far he couldn't see when another woman was attractive. Marjorie didn't know for sure but she felt almost certain that John Smith's heart was thudding like her own; and that no matter how much they talked about inconsequential things, deep in his mind his thoughts matched her own. You could feel a thing like that. Any woman, with any natural instinct at all, knew when she had attracted a man.

THEY DROVE FOR about a half hour like this . . . it was almost an hour and a half back to the house. Then suddenly Marjorie turned off into a little side lane. She said, innocently, "My arms are tired. I'm going to rest a moment. Do you mind?"

John Smith said, evenly, "Everything you think I mind I find utterly to my intense liking."

Marjorie tried hard not to look elated. This was simply too perfect, John Smith falling for her like this. It would serve Daisy right if she kept John Smith away from the house until the last possible minute before the debut. And during the debut Daisy wouldn't have any time at all to get her clutches back into him. And after the debut, the whole house-party would be over. Daisy would go on home; John would go back to his office. For once in her life Daisy would be frustrated.

Marjorie tilted her golden head back, a little toward John's shoulder. Her lips lay like a quivering bow of scarlet very close to his own. John Smith looked down into her small lovely upturned face. For a moment his eyes left those scarlet lips, traveled downward and stopped abruptly on the delicious outward thrust of her bosom, and the gorgeous modeling of her lithe figure, accentuated as it was by the languid pose she had assumed. When he looked back into her eyes his own were burning.

With a little groan his lips ground down upon hers with a primitive intensity that snapped Marjorie's body taut with awakened sensitivity. Her bosom surged upward against his muscle-packed chest, boring into it. Bored and strained until his fingers crept under the mink cape and clutched her full round arm, pressing the silk of her dress into her skin and setting her tense nerves tingling with an even more thrilling response than she had known she was capable of.

Marjorie gasped when John's arm crept around her and his grip tightened about her waist and kneaded the softness beneath his finger tips. His breath was a flame against her parted lips.

John said into his kiss, "Look here, Marjorie, I don't seem to be able to stop myself."

He expected some sort of an answer, Marjorie knew . . . possibly a rebuke. But she couldn't do anything but cling to him. Eagerly, impatiently she placed her soft pink palms upon his dark cheeks and drew his face back to her own. Then as his hard lips crushed down on her own she strained against him, so close that they seemed to be fused into one throbbing body.

Marjorie's head fell back across the back of the seat with a little moan. The pulse in her throat was quick and hot and painful. Revenge, she had always been led to suppose, was a decidedly sorry business. But this . . . oh, my dear this . . . ! She remained there then in a sort of blissful daze, one part of her mind trailing along with John's caressing fingers, the other deliciously conscious of the movement of his lips on her throat above the

bare V of her blouse. And presently with his lips back on her own, Marjorie came awake, her whole eager young body meeting pressure with pressure, kiss with kiss.

A LONG WHILE LATER with her head on John's shoulder Marjorie heard a rumbling noise on the highway. She heard it as if through a dream. And then suddenly she sprang upright. "The three o'clock bus!" gasped Marjorie in a kind of wail. She pushed John away, ran a cursory comb through her golden hair. She turned the car quickly out of the lane and sped up the road at a dizzy speed. John Smith said in a rather plaintive tone:

"Well—out with it. What's the connection? You hear the three o'clock bus and you suddenly go berserk. Is it a family weakness?"

"The three o'clock bus," said Marjorie, evenly, "means that it's nearly three o'clock."

"So what?" said John Smith.

"So I've got to get back in time to make my debut. We're an hour and a half from there now. I've got to make it in an hour."

Neither of them spoke for some time after that. The speedometer wavered skittishly between sixty and seventy. The hands of the clock sped fiendishly. Marjorie prayed there wouldn't be any cops along the way. Only ten miles more. . . .

Suddenly John Smith said, "Look here . . . you're not crazy, are you?"

"No," said Marjorie, "of course not."

"But look here, we just passed the McCormack place a second ago. Why didn't you stop? Where are you taking me any way?"

"Didn't Daisy tell you you were coming to my debut? I'm Marjorie Jennings."

"And just who the hell is Daisy?"

"Don't you *know?*"

"No," said John Smith. "I don't. I know only that Bill McCormack invited me down for the week-end. They were having another guest or two. A couple of girls. Bill said he'd send one of 'em to meet me. I thought you were that girl!"

Marjorie pressed her foot on the brake. The car stopped abruptly swinging them toward the windshield. "Do you mean to say you're not John Smith?"

"Of course, I'm John Smith," said John Smith, "but I'm probably not the John Smith you went hunting for. They're a lot of us. Look at the telephone books if you don't believe me." And then suddenly John Smith was very serious. His dark eyes moved over Marjorie's face, closely, warmly. He said, "The right John Smith or the wrong one . . . I meant everything I said and did today. You believe that, don't you, Marjorie?"

Marjorie said, "Yes, John, I do. I meant it too. Though I don't think I was really sure of it until this minute." That was true. Daisy had spoiled the first John Smith—the real John Smith.

"Better late than never," said John Smith. And then, "And now I want to go with you to your house and watch you make your debut. Okay?"

Marjorie said, "Okay," but her heart was heavy. What would happen when Daisy set her two blue eyes on *this* John Smith?

MARJORIE WAS DRESSED now for the important role. A little flirt hat sat demurely atop her shining curls and her face above the shimmering white satin was innocently radiant. In the receiving line she shook hands with

(*Please turn to page* 64)

Blonde TROUBLE

"Out!" he yelled. "To me you're just a headache!"

SOMEBODY had been snooping around his room at the Palmetto Baths. Val Norton saw that as soon as he went in. Tall, bronzed from the winter Florida sun, the words *Life Guard* lettered in white across the front of his bathing shirt, Val stood surveying the place.

Nothing there to interest any crook. His framed diploma on the wall, his only suit of clothes in the closet, his battered valise under the bed—Val couldn't imagine who would take the trouble to sneak into his quarters.

He saw something in the corner and picked it up. It was a crumpled handkerchief, very tiny, very feminine and much scented. Val sniffed the exotic perfume before he narrowed his eyes and tucked it safely away. Then, with a shrug, he peeled off the suit he had worn all day on the beach and climbed into the clothes hanging in the closet.

It was nearly seven o'clock then. The baths were deserted. The beach stretched empty and desolate beyond the dunes. Val knew at this hour cocktails were in vogue at the fash-

By

Cliff Carruth

"Hardboiled, aren't you? Just what don't you like about me?"

ionable hotels at Point Sable, that orchestras were playing and evening gowns glittering in the soft afterglow.

He smiled thinly as he made his way toward the parking space and the roadster that had cost him $35 cash, a fortnight previous. His dinner would be consumed at the Gravy Boat, that busy cafeteria in town. His music would be the clatter of crockery and the swish of soup, going up and down.

As Val reached his drab and dusty car he stopped. Curled comfortably up in the front seat was a blonde girl. She was young, about eighteen or so, and she had the face of an angel. Her eyes were a deep topaz, her lips like ripe cherries, her figure gorgeous, as Val had reason to know.

She smiled languorously at him, her parted lips revealing a glimmering line of pearl. Val frowned, annoyed. He knew her. She was Sue Chappel, daughter of the wealthy Chappels who inhabited the big, tile-roofed villa on the lagoon.

For the two weeks of his job at the baths, this girl had bothered him. She wouldn't let him alone. She had pursued him in a fashion strange and mysterious. She had tried in every possible way to arouse his interest in her. Continued failure, evidently, had not discouraged her in the slightest.

"Burning up?" she inquired coolly.

"What's the idea?" Val asked.

"Nothing much. I'm going to dinner with you."

"Oh, yeah? Try another shot. You're going to dinner but—not with me, baby!"

Her reply was to relax comfortably against the tattered leather upholstery and continue to smile dreamily at him. She wore a cute little white silk dress. It was practically backless and, Val decided, she didn't have any too much on under it.

Her rounded bosom made a mockery of a brassiere as a covering or shield. Her hips were smoothly curved under the clinging silk and her full, cherry lips were sensuous in their carmine smile. Val had seen her every day in the brief bathing suit she wore for her sunbaths. How she got away, unashamed with it, was a question. Up North, he knew, a suit like Sue's on any respectable beach would immediately lodge its wearer in jail.

"C'mon, climb out," he said curtly. "I'm in a hurry."

"I'm not," she replied drowsily. "I've got all day—and night."

Val drew his brows together. His handsome face darkened. He'd had about enough of Sue Chappel, sufficient blonde trouble to last a long while. With an effort he kept his temper in check.

"What are you trying to do—see how much I'll take?" he asked roughly. "Why don't you leave me alone? I've shown you plainly I'm not interested in you. You're not my type and I'm not yours. Scram, like a good kid."

"In two days," she said placidly, "it'll be the twenty-sixth of the month."

"So what?"

"So you've got to be interested in me!" she told him.

"Nuts! I don't want to be rude, but I think you're a little touched!"

"Simply got to!" she repeated slowly. "I made up my mind to that when I first saw you. You're just the kind of a man I like best. You're big, strong and oh, so masculine! And I know you're not married or engaged or even burned up about any other girl. So, you see, that makes it one hundred percent as far as I'm concerned."

As usual she was speaking in riddles. Val lost his patience. Opening the roadster's right door he reached in and hauled her off the seat. She struggled, but to no avail. When he got her out Val secretly thrilled to the soft warmth of her in his arms.

When he looked down he saw the deep cleft under the bras and her creamy, delicately tanned skin. To save his life he couldn't help feel a funny tingle surge through him. Hastily he set her upright on small, shapely feet that were supported by a pair of delightfully curved legs, unstockinged and as brown as the legs of a beachcomber.

Val kicked the starter and backed swiftly out. Sue Chappel stood where he had put her. Her odd eyes focused on him speculatively. A stain of pink tinted each smooth cheek.

"I'm not through!" she called after him, as he grinned at her and waved a hand. "You'll see—"

After his cafeteria meal Val wandered around town. The recollection of Sue in his arms stirred him queerly. He couldn't put it away from him. How soft she had been, how delectably warm! What had she meant by mentioning the 26th of the month? Was she a trifle balmy—*what?*

The round, white moon was up when Val finally drove back to the baths, put the car up and walked down the planked promenade toward the building where he had his room. He had taken no more than a few long strides before he came to a quick halt, his gaze on the moonlit beach.

There, where the frothy combers broke, a

slim, familiar figure stood, arms outstretched. She wore the same scanty suit he had mentally condemned as indecent. The glow of the moon turned her young body to silver and her hair to platinum.

Val suppressed an exclamation. Rigidly he watched while she ran into the swirling surf, dove through a breaking wave and started to swim. Val's lean face hardened. The damn little fool—she wasn't any too hot as a swimmer! What was the idea of her trying it out when there was no one around to render first aid if she got in a jam?

Further and further—Val's frown turned to a worried expression. Where was she headed—for Scotland? He vaulted the rail lightly and ran down to the surf line.

"Hey! Come back! You're out too far!"

His bellow must have reached her. She saluted him with a high flung arm before she buried her face in the sea again. Val didn't hesitate. Off went trousers, coat and shirt. He knew the treachery of the tide when it was on the turn. She might want to commit suicide but he wasn't going to let her spoil his clean record for him.

POWERFUL STROKES CARRIED him to her in the wave-tossed trough of the ocean. He ranged 'longside and grabbed her arm.

"Leave me alone!" she panted.

"You're coming in—*now!*"

"That's what you think! I'm—"

She tried to pull her arm free. Val wasn't in any mood for argument. He employed the same tactics he used in emergency cases—when a swimmer was drowning.

A clout on the chin took all the fight from her. Val caught her as she let go. He got an arm around her slender waist and headed back to the shore.

She had undressed in the space between the locker rooms and the dryer. Her clothes were in a little pile there, the slinky brassiere impudently on top. Val gave her a final shake and pushed her against the brick wall.

"I'm going to complain to the authorities about you! You're the worst pain in the neck I've ever known! You're a menace! Get dressed and get out of here!"

A seductive smile, slow and amorous, curved her petal-red lips. She ran a hand down over the sweeping line of her plane-flat torso and swelling hips. Val breathed harder. The scanty one-piece suit had become disarranged from his long haul back through the pounding surf.

The narrow straps holding it bracelet fashion about her neck had slipped. Her breasts were more revealed than concealed—gelatinous mounds with a sensuously provocative movement when she stirred. The water had made the rest of what little material there was cling tightly to her. In the molten flood of the sailing moon she appeared nearly unclad and Val's pulses beat faster as he realized that.

"Well, you had to come out and get me anyway!" she said cheerfully. "You must like me—some. You wouldn't let me drown."

"I was thinking of my job!" Val said crisply. "It's my business to keep people from drowning! I'm a life saver, in case you've forgotten."

"And the flavor doesn't matter," she wisecracked. "You're sweet and—ever so cute in your shorts!"

FOR THE FIRST TIME VAL remembered his own abbreviated costume. With a smothered exclamation he wheeled and beat it down to where he had left his outer clothing.

When he returned Sue was struggling into the white silk dress. It was halfway over her yellow head and Val had an unobstructed view of her flimsy step-ins, the round garters holding her stockings aloft, and the silly bras that in no way protected the charming double burden filling their cups to overflowing.

"Help me, can't you?" she said in a muffled tone.

Val yanked the dress into place and handed her her white handbag.

"Good night and—*out!*"

"Hardboiled, aren't you?" she observed. "Tough guy!" Her voice sank, a wheedling note creeping into it. "Why can't you act regular? Any other man—"

"Yeah, I know. Any other man would have had you in his arms days ago. But I'm not 'any other' man. I'm me and you're a headache."

"Just what don't you like about me?" she inquired.

"Everything! I think you're crazy! You're rich and I'm a poor lug trying to get by. You want amusement, somebody to romance with. Well, you've picked the wrong party, baby. I'm a serious somebody and I don't waste time fooling around with janes who want a good time and then, when they get it, drop me like a hot cake!"

"Oh," she cried softly, "so you want matrimony—the fireside, slippers and stuff. You expect—"

"Beat it!" Val requested curtly. "I've got to lock up for the night."

He turned on his heel and left her without further comment. Val did his routine duty. After he checked on the various doors to make certain they were locked he went back and found Sue had gone. Only a damp puddle was a souvenir of where she had stood.

Val sat down and smoked a thoughtful cigarette. A dreamy sense of tropical languor possessed him. Against his better judgment, his logic, he felt intrigued. Perhaps he was an idiot for passing up Sue Chappel. He could not seem to figure things out. He was confused, upset.

It was close to midnight when Val sought his room. In darkness he opened the door, went in and shut and locked it after him. He took a forward step across the matting and stopped as quickly as if he'd been shot.

Curled up in his bed, the sheets drawn to her chin, her blonde hair awry on the pillow, Sue Chappel reclined! She made no pretense of sleeping. Her long lashed eyes looked at him silently as Val switched on the tiny light beside the bed.

"Now I'm mad!" he said through set teeth. "This is the last straw!"

Grimly he turned to the washstand across the room. There was bowl and pitcher there. The latter vessel was filled with half a gallon of cold water. Val reached for it.

Watching him, Sue suddenly flung the sheet aside and sat bolt upright. In lieu of a nightie she wore the brassiere and panties. She registered alarm when he walked back, carrying the pitcher.

"Hey! What are you gonna do! You can't do—"

Swish!

Val aimed and fired. The half gallon shot accurately from the pitcher's wide-lipped mouth and doused Sue. She gave vent to a startled, strangled cry and spluttered, looking like a drowned mouse. Rubbing her eyes indignantly she did the exact opposite of what Val intended for her.

Sue sat down on the wet bed, pushing her damp yellow hair aside from her moist face.

"Just for that," she grated, "I'll never go!"

"Oh, yes, you will! And now!"

He caught her in his arms. His strength was too much for her puny efforts to resist. Val picked her up. It was a new experience for him and one not without emotional effects.

For a minute she fought desperately. The brassiere went askew, her wet hair hung limply. Val tried to force her to the door. She wound her legs about his to prevent and her arms tightened about his neck.

"Val!"

The plea in her low cry made him stand still. He looked at her, breathing hard. Her quivering lips were only inches from his own, her breath fanned his hot face and the twin hills of her breasts jammed themselves hard against his chest.

"What—what is it?"

Suddenly she began to cry. Two trembling tears, large as jewels, appeared on the long lashes, hesitated, rolled down her satiny cheeks. That was too much for Val. He could stand abuse, being bothered and annoyed and wise-cracks, but tears were his undoing.

"Sue!"

"Oh, Val, dear! You're so mean and I—I love you so much!"

Something happened to Val. Within he felt a snap—then a pounding rush of blood in his veins and a clamorous excitement that filled him with a strange savage tenderness. Hardly aware of what he did he brought his mouth close to hers. Their lips met and clung and Val, dizzy and weak, heard what he was telling her:

"I—I guess I've loved you ever since you first—first started to bother me! But what's the use, darling! You're—"

Her red lips parted and her bosom rose and fell, making the brassiere slip further. Her eyes, too, changed. The pupils dilated and the eyes glowed with a soft, wonderful light.

"I know who you are!" she whispered. "I sneaked in here this afternoon. I saw your law school diploma on the wall, some of the

(*Please turn to page 63*)

Private Demonstration

Mr. Gale: "Your sister was shocked by the way I kissed you last night."

Miss Calm: "Oh, so she peeked?"

Mr. Gale: "No, but while you were upstairs getting your hat and coat I showed her how I kiss you!"

LOOK BEFORE YOU LOVE

By ARTHUR WALLACE

THE letter from her father had been long and very explicit. Connie recalled excerpts from it as she settled herself in her pullman seat and prepared for the long, overnight ride to the city.

"You might just as well come in at once . . . from all reports you're getting nothing out of college . . . that last escapade was disgraceful. I want you to meet young Gordon Grange who is now on the way to being a successful lawyer . . . it has always been my hope that our families would unite. . . . "

And so on—for five closely typewritten pages. Connie sighed and gazed out at the bleak, cheerless country through which the train was running.

That last escapade. There had been so many collegiate escapades she couldn't remember which was which. Dad probably meant the statue escapade. That was something! Connie smiled as she thought of it. At the moment she couldn't recall whose brilliant idea it had been. It all seemed to crystallize spontaneously.

The founder of the college had set up a dozen Greek statues all over the campus. Both male and female. The night after a football victory, some of the Delta Mu girls and some of the Tau Epsilon boys, intoxicated with the team's success—and a few cocktails—decided to pose in the postions of the Greek works of art.

Connie had chosen a particularly voluptuous marble lady to emulate. The lady was almost nude. To make it realistic, Connie divested herself of most of her clothes and struck an heroic posture.

It was grand fun until the photographer for the local newspaper, having gotten wind of what was going on, took a flashlight picture of Connie and the statue—both in their abbreviated suits.

The Tau Epsilon boys had mobbed the picture-taker and relieved him of his camera. Someone got the plate, spirted it away and developed it. Prints began to circulate around the college. There were calls to the Dean's office . . . denials . . . reverberations. Fortunately, the face on the picture was blurred. But the body wasn't. Nobody who knew Connie could mistake the figure. Those high, pointed breasts and the Venus-like sweep of hips were individual.

Connie sighed. Well, it had been grand fun while it lasted. Now she wondered what her Dad had in store for her. Gordon Grange was one thing. She had been hearing about the Granges of California ever since she was knee-high. It seems her grandfather and Gordon Grange's grandfather had prospected in the Yukon and pledged all for one and one for all. It was very melodramatic and sentimental but it bored Connie to tears.

She glanced across the aisle and noticed a recent copy of a magazine on the seat opposite her. She hadn't thought to buy any reading matter before getting on the train and was no telling when a news butcher would come through. Certainly, whoever was occupying the seat wouldn't object to her borrowing the magazine. She reached over for it and began thumbing through the pages.

She was engrossed in a humorous article when a pleasantly modulated voice said: "Funny, isn't it?"

Connie looked up. A tall, broad shouldered young man with clean-cut features and smiling brown eyes was standing next to her seat. He had a football player's build and an Arrow collar ad face.

"Oh, is—is this your magazine?" she gulped. "I—I forgot to buy one and—"

"That's quite all right," he said. "I'm finished with it. Dull day, isnt' it?"

Connie reacted favorably to his appearance. He was the type of man every college girl dreamed about dating. She felt her breasts trembling in the net cups of her brassiere. Funny little sensations trickled across her smooth, sensitive body.

"Terribly dull," she replied, smiling up at him and spreading her arms, the result was

that he could see the twin globes under her tight, high-necked sweater.

"Good day for a drink," he said. "Would you be interested? The Club Car is rather nice."

Connie rose, dropped the magazine and smoothed out her skirt. "I'd love it. There's nothing I hate more than riding a train by myself."

In the Club Car, they both ordered Scotch and soda. "I suppose we should introduce ourselves to one another," he said. "My name is Dick Templar."

Connie extended her hand. "Connie Reeves. We can drop last names, can't we and just be Dick and Connie?"

He took her hand. "Agreed."

They were on their second drink when Connie nudged him. "How do you like the blonde across the aisle?" she whispered.

He looked at Connie's dark hair. "Personally, I prefer brunettes."

"You're just talking. Isn't she something or other? Don't men go for that exotic type?"

The platinum blonde to whom Connie was referring was seated across the aisle in the company of a short, swarthy-faced man whose ebony hair was plastered flat against his skull. He wore spats and a huge diamond ring. The blonde was garbed in a dull gold lame cocktail dress just a little too tight for her overflowing figure.

"Just one good breath and she will pop out," Connie said.

The swarthy little man looked over at Connie and smiled. Something made Connie smile back. Pure, unadulterated devilishness. Dick noticed it.

"Tit for Tat," he said, under his breath.

"Go ahead," Connie murmured. "She looks like torrid stuff."

Suddenly the swarthy little man rose and crossed the aisle. The creases in his trouser legs were razor sharp. He bowed before Connie.

"I wonder, perhaps, whether you would care to play a rubber or two of bridge?" His voice was smooth and oily.

Connie looked at Dick. "Would you?"

He shrugged. "If you wish."

The little man rubbed his hands. "Good, I'll have a table set up. My name is Michael Delano." He indicated the over-voluptuous blonde. "That's Mrs. Delano. Everyone calls us Mike and May. A few rubbers of bridge will while away the time, won't it?"

Dick introduced Connie and himself. The table was set up and Mrs. Delano joined them. On closer inspection, Connie decided she had never seen a woman with so much make-up on her face before. The blonde's lips were caked with color and her eyelashes hung with beads of mascara.

Two hours later, when the last call for dinner was announced, Dick pushed his chair back from the table. Both he and Connie had been drinking too much. Connie's cheeks were flushed and her eyes were bright as diamonds.

"How much are we out?" he asked.

Mike Delano computed some figures. "Only $63.00. We can continue after dinner in our compartment. It's more comfortable there. Compartment 22. We'll meet you after dinner."

Dick and Connie went out on the observation platform for a breath of air. "They took us to the cleaners," Connie said. "It was all my fault. I played horrible bridge."

"No, you didn't."

She turned to him and put her hands on his shoulders. "I did so. I'm going to pay all the losses." Her hips swayed and her body undulated with the motion of the train. "You don't like that blonde, do you?"

"Of course not."

"She was trying to make you." The train went around a curve and Connie lost her balance. Dick's arm swung around her waist and held her close against him.

He could feel the swell of her breasts and the undulating curve beneath them. "So what?"

Connie's fingers rippled over his shoulders. "Do you like me?"

"Yes." The palm of his hand was hot through her sweater.

"How much?"

"Must I measure it?"

Connie's heart was fluttering madly. No man had ever made her feel like this before. Maybe the drinks were partly responsible. She had the urge to do something utterly unconventional; something daring. She did it . . . suddenly. She came up on the tips of her toes and jammed her moist, parted lips against his mouth in a kiss that left no question as to its passionate intensity.

At the same time, her arms curled about his neck and she glued her curved body to his. It was a long kiss—as kisses go. Connie's breath was far from unhurried when she finally brought it to an end.

"I—I had to do that!" she gasped.

Dick removed a handkerchief and wiped the carmine smear from his lips. "Do you have to do it with every man you meet?"

Connie's eyes blazed. "Are you insinuating that—" The words choked up inside her. She turned on her heel, yanked the door open and almost ran down the aisle.

Dick didn't follow. He stood there, watching her hips swing as though they were on ball-bearing rollers. He was smiling enigmatically.

Later, when he stepped into the dining car, Connie was seated with the Delanos. He nodded and smiled as he passed the table. The Delanos returned the smile but Connie's eyes were directed at her empty soup bowl.

Dinner over, Dick went back to his seat. Connie's was empty. He waited a half hour or so, became impatient. The compartment cars, he learned from a conductor, were up ahead.

Before he knoked at the door of Number 22, he made certain someone was in. He heard voices—the blonde's husky, rasping voice, her husband's oily tones and Connie's tinkling laughter. Then he knocked.

Mike Delano opened the door. "Oh, we were wondering about you. Come in."

Dick saw Connie with a highball glass in her hand. Her eyes were glazed. She had evidently been drinking heavily.

"I've come to pay the money we owe you," he said, reaching for his wallet. "It was sixty-three, wasn't it?"

Mike Delano waved a manicured hand. "No hurry, no hurry. Let's play a few more rubbers."

"I don't care to play any more."

Connie laughed. "He's afraid I might lose for him. He's yellow."

Dick colored. "Maybe I will play," he said evenly.

A porter came in and set up a table. Mike Delano poured Dick a drink which remained untouched. Consistently, the Delanos held marvelous cards. Rubber after rubber went by with Connie's and Dick's losses piling up. Finally Connie threw her cards down.

"I can't see straight," she mumbled, lurching over to one side.

Mike Delano caught her in his arms, lifted her up and sat her down on one of the green plush seats. "You're all right, baby," he said, running his hand over her hips and cuddling her so that she was leaning against his arm.

May Delano got up and came around to where Dick was seated at the table. "How about you and me going out for a breath of air, handsome?" She dropped her ruby-tipped fingers on his shoulder, ran them under the lapel of his jacket. Leaning over him, her big breasts swung out like over-ripe fruit.

Dick rose. The blood rushing to his head. Mike Delano was caressing Connie openly now, taking advantage of her muscular anesthesia to caress her.

"Keep your hands off her, Delano!"

The big blonde stepped in front of him and tried to swing her arms around his neck. The pupils of her bluish eyes were hot and dilated.

"Come on, Big Boy," she cooed. "Let's you and me—"

Dick pushed her aside. His long arm shot out and his fingers fastened in the collar of Delano's jacket. He lifted the man up and shook him like a terrier shakes a rat. Something happened that he hadn't anticipated. Playing cards fell out of Delano's sleeves and fluttered to the floor.

For a moment Dick saw scarlet. So, that was the game? Card sharps! He set Delano on his feet and landed a short, fast punch to the point of his jaw. He went down and out.

It must have looked peculiar to passengers and trainmen alike to see a big, strapping young man carrying a limp girl through the entire line of cars to the observation platform. But, funny or not, Dick got Connie out into the brisk open air and propped her up in a chair.

He sat next to her, his arm supporting her back and her head resting on his shoulder. "You little dummy," he said softly, kissing her lips.

Connie didn't move. Dick felt the beat of her heart under the roundness of a resilient breast.

"You need someone to keep you under control," he said, caressing her gently.

In the darkness, Dick couldn't see her eyelids flutter. Neither could he see the faint smile on her lips. Minutes went by and with each passing one, Dick's lips became better acquainted with hers.

Finally, Connie came to. She sat up with a start. "What—what happened?" she gasped.

"They were card sharps. Instead of paying him money I paid him with a punch."

"But—but what happened to me? How did I get here?"

"You passed out and I carried you. Now,

(*Please turn to page 60*)

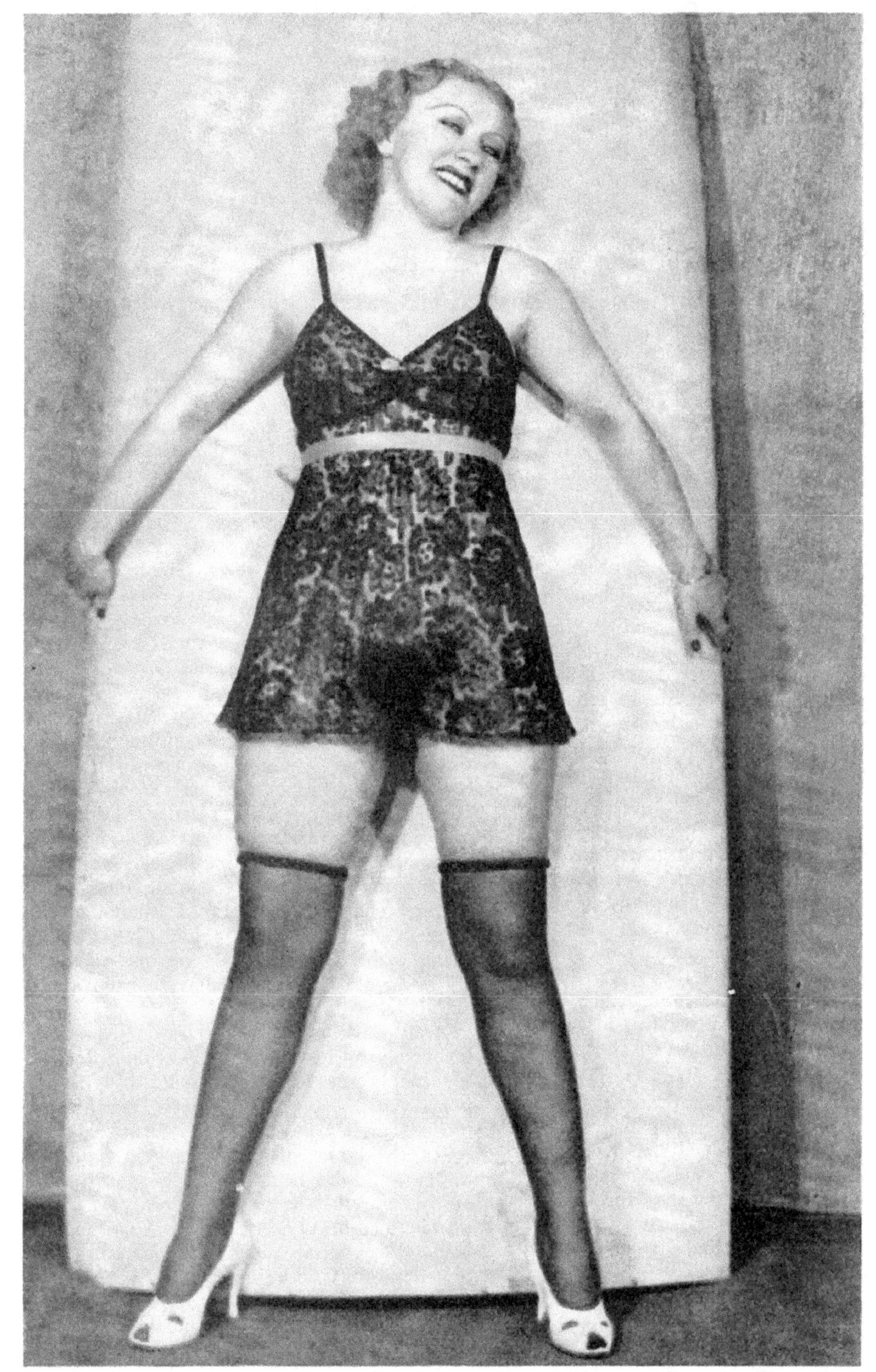

SONG AT EVE

By

TOM KANE

IT WAS only a joint, really, but you'd think by the way Russ O'Keefe was dressed and by his manner generally that it was the Rainbow Room at least.

He sat on his spine at the desk, his feet on the blotter and his good looking face swathed in an aura of expensive cigarette smoke. His full dress suit had set him back two hundred dollars and he was very proud of it. He did not move when the knock came at the door. He merely said, "Come in and let it go at that.

"You wanted to see me, Russ?"

"Come in, Andy. I sure did. Come in and close the door after you."

Andrea Weeks, blonde, outwardly calm and scandalously dressed entered the little office slowly and closed the door. She looked at Russ and he looked at her. Neither said anything.

Slowly the blood crept to Andy's soft cheeks. Russ was frankly undressing her with his eyes and owing to what she was wearing the job was not very difficult one.

Her white satin evening gown was cut to display as much of her lush young body as possible. Her shoulders, arms and back were bare and it was all Andy could do to keep the two thin pieces of material between her high, round breasts and the eyes of anyone looking at her. Her waist was slender but her hips wide and flaring. Russ had insisted that she wear no girdle, and when she moved it was very exciting.

"Come over here," Russ ordered. Andy did so. Russ reached for her and slipped his arm about her waist. His hand, in the center of her bare back was hot and Andy could not help the little thrill that shot through her.

"What's on your mind, Russ?" she asked and she did what she could to keep her voice cool and casual.

Russ grinned and his grip tightened. His fingers started to knead the yielding flesh of her back and he was gazing avidly at the lush curves of Andy's almost exposed figure.

"You and I aren't getting anywhere in a great hurry," Russ said.

"I told you that, you know," Andy said. "I told you that when you gave me the job with the band."

Russ' eyes snapped, and he dropped his long legs to the floor. Before Andy realized it, she was on his lap and the low neckline of the gown was gaping. Russ could see the tops of her lovely breasts and his eyes glittered.

"Listen, toots," he said and his voice was harsh. "This has been going on long enough. Either you come through or you get the hell out of the band."

Andy smiled. "So we've come to it at last," she said. The smile faded and she eyed Russ coldly. No longer did his nearness do anything to her and she knew that he could have jammed her up tight against him but as far as she was concerned, nothing would have happened to her.

"You listen to me," she continued. "Until this moment I couldn't make up my mind between you and Bobby Dukes. Bobby Dukes wins and I don't care if he loses his job, too."

Russ' eyes were hard. "So you're going to turn me down in favor of a lousy piano player. You must be crazy. I admit that this place is pretty much of a joint, but I'm not going to be here always. One of these days I'll be in the money. I'll have a band at the best hotel in town."

Andy made an effort to rise but Russ held her firmly on his lap. "It fakes no difference to me," she said. "When I go for a man . . . . I go for a *man,* not his job nor his money. When're we through?"

Russ did not answer. His grip tightened on her and he held her close against him. Andy knew that he could see plenty of white, unconcealed beauty, but there was nothing she could do about it and so long as Russ contented himself with just looking she did not mind so much.

"Be decent," Russ said, and his voice was husky. "You know I'm crazy about you. Always have been."

"You take the dog, you're always telling me what a great lover of pets you are!"

"I can't, Russ," Andy said and her voice, too, was low. "I just can't."

THEN HE KISSED HER. Kissed her hard and the breath was forced from Andy's beautiful little body. Russ' hands seemed to be coals of fire. She felt them in the small of her naked back, along the smooth flesh of her white upper arms and at her narrow waist. The backs of them brushed fleetingly and accidentally against the tips of her covered bosom as Russ' lips were burning against hers and she could feel the hammering of his heart through his stiff shirt. She struggled and managed to break his hold on her. She got to her feet. Her eyes were blazing and her breasts rose and fell.

"I'm going now," she panted. Russ rose also and stood over her.

"I do something to you," he said huskily. "Why not admit it? We can both be happy and you can reach the crest with me and the band."

"No. If there weren't Bobby . . . but there is. No, I can't do it, Russ."

Russ rubbed the back of a trembling hand across his eyes.

"All right," he said. "And you can keep your jobs. Both you and Bobby."

Andy smiled and came towards him. The lights shone in the yellow curls on her head and her eyes twinkled. "Thanks," she said. "But we'll go at the end of the week. It'll be better that way."

Russ shrugged his padded shoulders. "That's up to you." He glanced at his watch. "We'd better go."

ARM-IN-ARM, ANDY AND BOBBY Dukes left the cheap little dance hall and walked to the corner. Bobby looked more like a football player than a piano player, and he was carelessly dressed and did not wear a hat. His hair was dark and curly and his face was ruggedly good looking.

At the corner they paused and Bobby grinned down at Andy.

"Where to?" he asked. "I know the answer. 'Take me home, Bobby. Take me home to Mother'."

Andy smiled up into his eyes. "For once you're wrong," she said. "We're going to do what you've always wanted me to do. We're going to take a look at those famed etchings of yours."

Color rushed to Bobby's face. "Andy!" His grip on her arm tightened and he drew her to him. "Does that mean that you've fallen in love with me?"

"Looks like it, Bobby. Sure does."

"Andy, that's just like you. All the time we've been working and making a few dollars you wouldn't have much to do with me. Now that we're through on Saturday . . . you tell me that you love me."

"It's because I love you that we're through on Saturday," Andy said.

"I get it. We'll take a cab and to hell with the subway."

They were pretty silent during the ride uptown. They sat close, almost touching and each was breathing heavily. It was Bobby who finally broke the silence.

"Know why I'm not kissing you?" he asked.

"Because you don't want to, I guess."

"It's because I wouldn't be able to stop at just kissing you."

Andy snuggled closer. "You'd be surprised if you knew how much I wanted you to kiss me."

"Don't. You're killing me."

Andy slipped her soft little hand into his and her fingers did this, that and the other. "Stop it," Bobby said hoarsely.

PRESENTLY THE CAB STOPPED and they alighted. Bobby paid the driver and a few seconds later, he swung open the door of his small, attractively furnished apartment. Andy entered and Bobby closed and locked the door.

"It's nice, Bobby," she said. "Very nice."

"Let me have your things."

Andy removed her wrap and she was still dressed in the scandalous evening gown. Bobby came to her and crushed her in his arms. Andy clung to him, flattening her lovely breasts against his rumpled shirt front. She jammed her body against his and her bare arms went slowly about his neck.

"Bobby," she whispered, "I want you to know that you're the first and only man I've ever loved."

"And I want you to know that you're the only girl in the world." He kissed her and it was as though waves of powerful electricity were being shot through them. They stiffened and then clung, shuddering, to each other. Andy's breasts were palpitating with emotion and as she clung to him it pressed them harder and harder against Bobby's chest. His hands were in the thick waves of her yellow hair, on the bare flesh of her pulsating back and slightly south of her flaring hips. When they

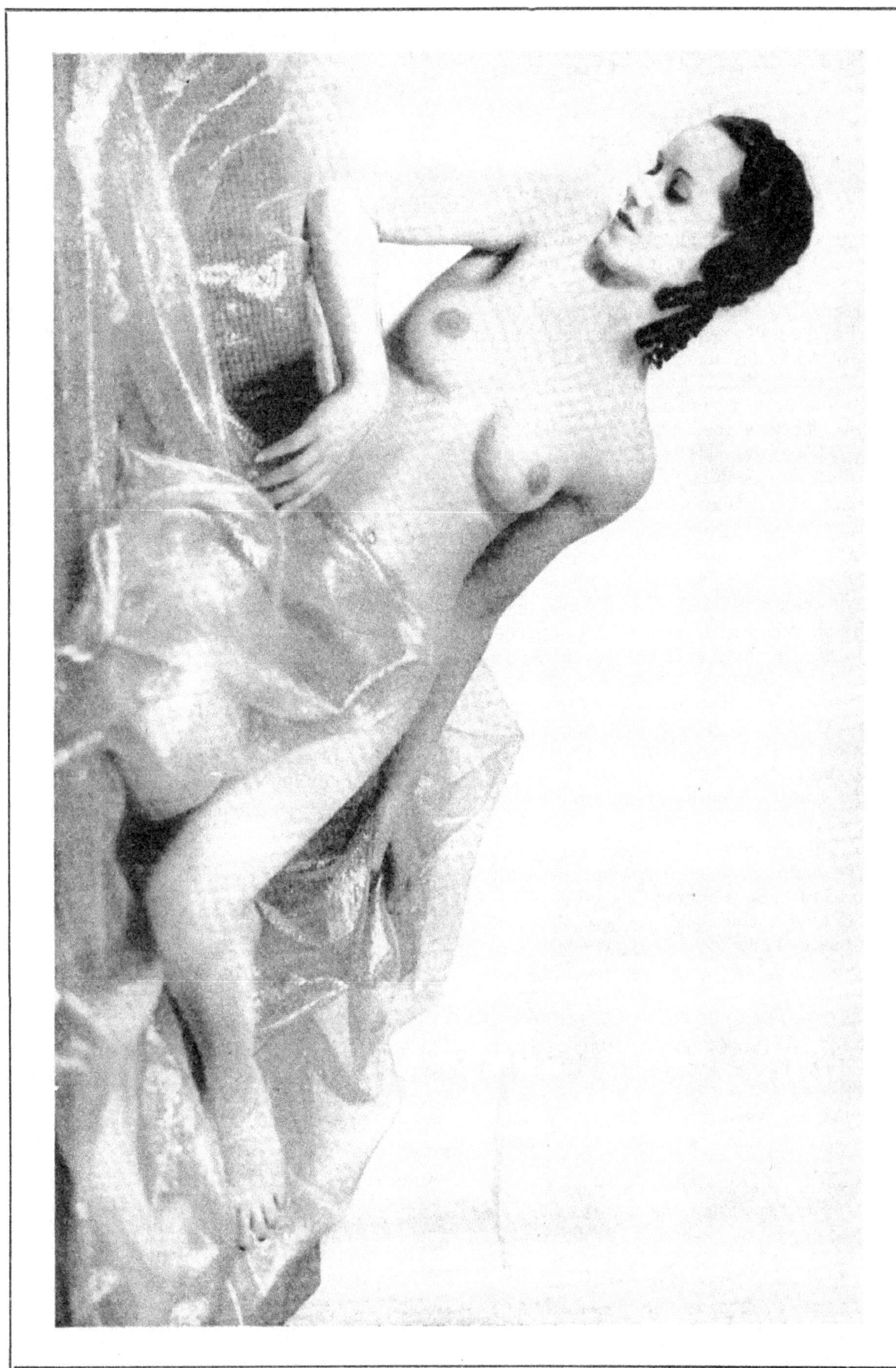

finally broke apart, they were both breathing heavily and their eyes were sparkling.

"Andy," Bobby said. "I want you to sing for me."

"Yes. What shall I sing?"

"A song I wrote myself. I wrote it for you. But, look . . ."

Bobby turned out all the lights save the one tiny one above the small piano. Then he came to Andy and reached for her, his fingers caught in the hooks at the side of the scandalous gown and it came open and cascaded to her feet. Andy crossed her bare arms across her breasts and faced him. She was dressed in sheer lingerie and high-heeled slippers. Bobby unpinned her yellow hair and allowed it to fall about her gleaming shoulders. Then he took her by the hand and led her to the piano. He sat down and Andy leaned over his shoulder.

"I can't sing," she whispered. "I'm all choked up."

"So'm I. Sing, Andy. Take the lead-sheet and read the lyrics. You take the release and sing it from then on."

Bobby started to play and he did not look at the keys. He never took his eyes off Andy as she stood, bosom heaving, holding the sheet of paper. He thought she was the most beautiful thing he had ever seen, and all his great love for her went into his playing of the song he had written. He reached the release and Andy's haunting voice took up the words.

Diminishing chords . . . silence. Bobby got to his feet and Andy almost fell into his arms.

"Marvelous," he muttered.

Andy clung to him and she was shuddering. "Bobby, Bobby, Bobby . . ."

Then she was swept off her feet into his arms . . .

OUT OF THE GLOOM CAME Andy's velvet voice. "There's a fortune in that song, Bobby."

"I think so, too, but how to get it? If I take it down to Tin Pan Alley, they'll steal it."

"I have it," and Andy's voice was a little drowsy. "Archie Hale's the man to see. If he sings it on one of his broadcasts, the song's made."

"Try and see Archie Hale."

"I know all about him. He likes the ladies, but he's one hundred per cent honest. There's only one thing he likes more than the ladies and that's money. You leave it to me, Bobby."

"I'd be willing to give him a piece of the song."

"Leave it to me, Bobby."

SYLVIA PICKED UP HER tray of cigarettes and looked Andy over for the last time.

"You'll do," she said. "In fact you're so beautiful, I don't know but what you'd make a better hat-check girl than I."

Andy smiled. "You're a peach, Sylvia," she said. "It's nice to know that one has real friends when one needs them."

"Here comes Archie now," Sylvia said. "You just leave everything to me."

Archie Hale and another man came up to the check room and tossed their hats and coats on it. They were about to turn away when Archie caught sight of Andy and grinned.

"Hello, Gorgeous," he said. "You're new, aren't you?"

"New, but not fresh," Andy said haughtily

Archie leaned over the counter. "Aw, don't be that way. I won't eat you."

Andy's eyes flashed. "Nothing you could do to me would interest me."

"That's what you think. How about a date, baby?"

"Go peddle your papers."

Archie grinned and patted Andy's hand. "We're going to get along fine," he predicted. Then, quite pleased with himself, he joined his friend at the luncheon table.

"Sylvia says you havn't a hope, Archie," his friend said.

"Archie says different," Archie said. "There's a look in that little girl's eye and I can read looks. That little lady and I're going to have breakfast together before long."

"Says you."

"Says me."

ANDY OPENED THE DOOR of Bobby's apartment and in the hallway, there stood Archie. Archie was holding his hat in his hand and he was grinning.

"Hello, Gorgeous," he said. "How about coming in?"

Andy smiled and stepped aside. Archie entered the apartment and removed his coat. He flung it to the back of a chair and faced Andy.

"That was a cute idea of yours," he said. "Sticking that note in the hatband of my hat. I thought you were going to be hard to make."

"I thought so, too," Andy said. "But then I saw you close up and I was sunk."

Archie grinned. There was something so boyish, so naive about him that he did not even offend and it was all Andy could do to keep herself from laughing in his face.

"Nice little place you've got here," Archie said. "How many rooms?"

"There isn't another. That's a day-bed over there."

"But this is night," Archie said.

Andy came to him and stood close. Archie looked down at her lovely hair and the perfume of it sent the blood coursing through his veins.

"Listen, Archie, if I give you a little thrill, will you promise me on your word of honor you won't put a finger on me until I say you can?"

Archie's eyes clouded over suspiciously. "What's the gag?" he demanded.

"Promise and I'll tell you."

"Listen, Beautiful, there isn't a girl in this town can say that Archie Hale ever took advantage of her. I'm probably the most honest man you'll ever meet on Broadway."

."That's what I've always heard. So how about the promise?"

"Sure, I promise."

Andy went over to the piano and arranged the lead-sheet of Bobby's song. Archie watched her curiously. Then she turned off all save the one little light over the piano. Then she faced Archie.

"Sit down at the piano," she commanded.

Wonderingly, Archie did as he was told. Instinctively, he looked the lead-sheet over and trailed his long, artistic fingers along the keyboard. Then he looked again at Andy.

She was standing in the center of the small room and her fingers were fumbling with the hooks at the sides of the gown she was wearing. Slowly, deliberately, her heart pounding and her breasts rising and falling, she slipped the dress over her head and tossed it to the back of a chair. Then, the shape and outline of her bosom just about visible in the gloom, she faced Archie. Archie half rose and Andy raised her hand.

"You promised," she reminded him.

Archie subsided. "That's right, I did."

"Play the number and I'll take it on the release."

With an obvious effort of will, Archie concentrated on the piano. He started to play, and gradually, as the number unfolded, his interest in Andy and her beauty lessened. He came to the release and Andy's warm, heartrending voice filled the small room. Archie glanced at her and smiled. But it was a professional smile of encouragement.

The number finished and Archie got to his feet. "Who wrote that?" he asked.

"Bobby Dukes, late pianist with Russ O'Keefe."

"Has it been published?"

"No, not yet."

Archie grabbed the lead sheet and stuffed it in his pocket. "It soon will be." He started for his hat and coat and Andy, devilishly, moved over to him. She crossed her arms over her bosom so that it was almost covered. Her head on one side, she said,

"You can kiss me if you want."

"Eh? Some other time, Gorgeous. Leave your phone number at the office and when I get a moment to spare . . . I've got to dash. There's dough—heavy dough—in this number."

In less than no time he was gone and Andy was at the telephone.

"Bobby? Hurry home. I'm waiting for you. Everything went off fine and the number's going to be published and to hell with us being fired. We'll be lousy with money. In the meantime . . . hurry home!"

Heart racing and eyes glowing, Andy flung herself on the couch full of joy at the success of her plan.

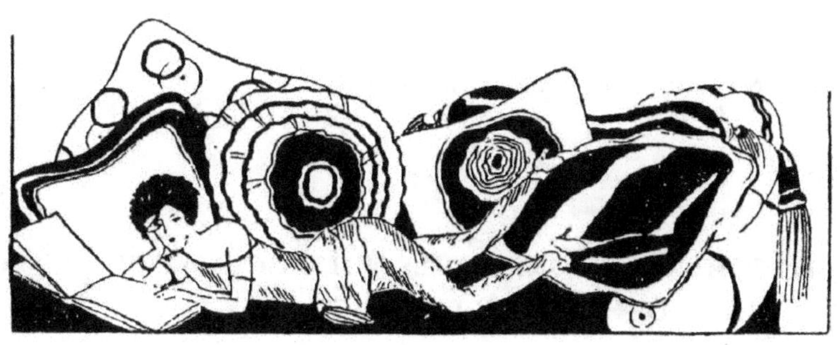

BURP: "*He sports around town most every night drinking 'Wild Women Cocktails'.*"

BWERP: "*Yeah, with his wife for a chaser.*"

* * *

1938 MODEL

Mary has a little lamb,
A pretty calf and toe,
But she'll have to show me more before
She claims me for her beau.

"Did you feel good last night?"

"No. She wouldn't let me!"

* * *

Blondie: "I hear that you had a little too much to drink when you were out with that nobleman last night."

Goldie: "Yeah, I was surely down for the count!"

* * *

WINNIE WINSOME SAYS SOME GIRLS WILL GO ANYWHERE FOR A MAN. OTHERS WILL GO FOR ANY MAN.

SOME HEELS . . . !

By

CLINTON HARCOURT

AS Lee Brice scurried backstage at the Amphion she saw Donny Reynolds wandering around, talking to himself. Lee knew that's what happened when you were putting on a show and only had a shoestring to work with, and no money in reserve.

Somewhere a whistle blew out on the apron of the deserted stage, a few lights came up and the voice of Oscar Wren sounded through his megaphone:

"Okay, girls. Take your places. We'll run over the first ensemble number. Ready, piano?"

Twenty or more young ladies frisked out from the wings. They were attired in all sorts of bizarre costumes, ranging from ordinary bathing suits to shorts and cotton shirts. They were a good looking flock. Trust Donny to pick the lookers, Lee thought. He always went for Beauty in the grand manner.

She had a specialty in what, at present, was the fourth scene and there was no hurry. Donny saw her and walked over. He was tall, thin from the nervous strain of seeking a bankroll, boyish and good looking. Once an ace hoofer in night clubs and what was left of vaudeville, he had spent a year in Hollywood, saved his jack and sunk it in the new musical venture.

" 'lo, Stylish. How about a smack-smack?"

"Don't you ever think about anything except kissing me?" Lee asked.

"Hardly ever. Listen. I want to see you later. Don't leave before you back-tap me, like a good kid."

"Okay," Lee nodded, and went on up to her dressing room.

She felt terribly sorry for Donny. He had bitten off more than he could comfortably roll on his molars. Lee knew what the show racket was, how you could drain dough into it by the fistful and see nothing but the need of more and still more before the first curtain rang up.

LEE'S THOUGHTS WANDERED. She thought about old Hy Gluckman while she stripped off her street clothes. Hy was a millionaire shoe manufacturer, with factories up in New England, and Hy, for months, had pursued her like the villain in a cheap melodrama. All Hy wanted was for her to come and be an ornament in his platinum-lined pent-house over on the East River.

In the mirror fronting her, Lee inspected her swelling, glamorous charms with critical approval. She didn't have to be egotistical to know she not only had what it took, but what was necessary for the take. Few on Broadway, or elsewhere, could boast such rounded, cone-tipped breasts, such a willowy, curved body, such marble thighs and seductive legs!

She stretched, still thinking how unfair it was that old Hy Gluckman had half the coin in the world and poor Donny not enough to float a musical piece with all the earmarks of being a box-office smash!

Once more she let her appraising glance wander over her lightly clad form. It rested on the decided fold that divided the heavy breasts and on the dimple-engraved tummy so flat from her dancing.

"Old Hy, the city slicker!" Lee murmured. "Baby needs booties—come you seven!"

Three hours later Donny handed her into a taxi and sank down beside her. It was mid-evening along the Gape Gorge and the lights made a rainbow pattern for the out-of-town buyers. Everywhere the movie houses had brilliant marquees.

Donny looked at them and sighed: "One musical in town and that doing an S.R.O. and lousy! People hungry for entertainment and me with a grand slam on my hands and not enough cash to go ahead. Show me a window and I'll show you some fancy diving!"

"Oh, cheer up," Lee said, rubbing her shoulder against his. "It never pours until it rains. You're not licked yet."

"Neither was Napoleon but they put him on the island just the same."

"Come on up to my place and I'll cook my

fur coat and we'll have a rabbit," Lee invited. "Right?"

"Where else did you think I was going?" Donny grinned feebly.

LEE HAD TWO rooms and one bath in the Sexy Sixties. It wasn't much of a place but it was warm and comfortable and that was something even if the divan springs were resting partially on the floor.

Donny scaled his hat to a table and sank down on the lumpy lounge. Lee shed her rabbit skin and ran her hands over her blue-black hair. Her brown eyes were very bright and sympathetic when she went for a decanter of rye and a flask of ginger-ale.

"Here's a shoulder," she said, pouring and mixing. "Go right ahead and cry your little eyes out."

"I've tried Wall Street, the movie magnets and I haven't gotten a tumble. Five grand—a buck in the dropet but it might as well be five million. Unless I get it before the fifteenth, when the Equity clamps, I'm all ironed out."

Lee took her glass over. "Five G's? There must be some way—"

"Yeah. That's what I thought. *You* tell *me.*"

"Mebbe," Lee murmured, "I could strike old Hy Gluckman, the rich shoe builder, for it. Hy's got a yen for me and—"

"Stop right there!" Donny's strong hand went over her mouth. "Look," he growled, "I know you could chisel the dough out of Hy, but I also know the price! Don't bring that up again, Lee, or I'm apt to foam at the teeth and break your furniture."

"But I thought—"

"Don't think!" He ran a quick arm around her lithe, young body. "Oh, Lee, this extravaganza meant so much to me. It meant *you!* Dough! A home—a bank account—and ten cent cigars!"

She let him draw her closer. She did like Donny more than any one man she had ever known. He had personality, charm, intelligence. He was sweet and he deserved success. She cuddled to him while, as usual, his hand caressed her, nestling in the warm hollow under her arm, wandering down to her slender waist and then retracing its course. And, as usual, tingles became delicious thrills and made her blood sing and her head swim rapturously.

"Donny—I wish you wouldn't."

"I gotta have something!" he said hoarsely. "I gotta have love—your love! Without that you might just as well get a broom and sweep me up and out!"

Then his lips found hers and clung. Lee kissed him with fervor and ardor born of thrills that kept mounting within her until her heart thumped like a Harlem drum and her pulses clamored madly. . . .

THE NEXT MORNING, towards eleven, Lee had breakfast on a card table in her living room. It consisted of toast and coffee, then more toast and more coffee. She could think of nothing but Donny and last evening—his arms and lips, kisses and the enchantment he inspired.

Abruptly, Lee drew a quick breath and reached for the telephone. She lighted a cigarette before she dialed a certain number, waited and spoke when the connection was made.

"Sato," she said, "is Mr. Gluckman home?"

"One minute, please. Find out." The voice grew bland. "This Miss Lee, please?"

"Yes, please," Lee said with faint humor.

Her heart stirred anticipatively while she waited, listening to far off voices. She coughed once or twice, either from the cigarette smoke or nervousness. Finally:

"Hello, Lee? Is that really you or is Sato trying to be smart?"

"It's me—I. Take your choice."

"Well, this is swell. I was thinking about you last night. Wondering what became of you."

"I thought," Lee told him, "I'd better wait for things to blow over. I mean, I'm sorry I clouted you that night. It wasn't what a lady would do."

Gluckman laughed. "Oh, that's forgotten. I was varnished anyway and deserved it. How about some lunch with me?"

"Elegant," Lee said quickly. "Same place, same time?"

He was waiting at the Dixie on 54th when Lee went into the foyer. Gluckman was tall, stout and ruddy faced. Gray shot through the black at his temples. His hair was growing thin on top, but he told Lee he didn't care because he never had liked fat hair. He had small, shrewd eyes and caressing hands that always made Lee think of a pair of matched hot water bottles.

A BACHELOR OF long standing, Gluckman was loose with his money when he wanted to be. He liked brunettes, particularly brunettes with perfect 36's and he liked Lee. Ever since he had sent her roses at the Hottentot, in her

floor show days and nights, he had been like a hound on the scent. The more Lee discouraged him the more he wanted her.

"This is lovely," Gluckman said, when they sat down. "Weather clear, track fast, beautiful gal. Go ahead, order anything."

Lee handed the menu to a waiting waiter. "All this and a cup of tea with lemon," she smiled.

"Ditto," Gluckman grunted. "But bring some champagne and make sure it's not excited cider."

Lee surveyed him dreamily. She was running contrary to Donny's wishes, but she had to do something and Hy was the something she was sure she could do, given half a Shanghai resident's chance. Five thousand bucks to him was like a subway ride to her.

"I need five G's," she said frankly, "to put in Donny's show. He's got a hit ready to break and he's cooked if he can't satisfy the Equity on next pay-day. How about it, want to invest?"

"Show business," Gluckman said, "is something I never fuss with."

"But you backed a drama once."

"Sure," he chuckled, "and that's why I'm cured."

"But if I assured you that you'd make a profit?"

"Lee," he went on, "if you swore on your grandma's grave I still wouldnt' be interested. However," he added slowly, "if *you* want five thou that, as Shakespeare used to say, is another story."

Lee's eyes narrowed. "How do you mean?"

He shrugged. "You know. Move out of your flat and into my pent-house. It's really charming, with the view and everything. The day you sail in is the day you get a payoff. I won't be crude about it either. I'll slip you the cash in some whimsical way that'll be perfectly delightful. Think it over and if you're interested let me know."

"It's the only out for me?" Lee asked.

"Coming *in*," he nodded, "is the only out!"

She swallowed some of the ice water in the tall goblet beside her. "Okay, I will think it over."

"Fond of this showboy, are you?"

The question was casual but Lee detected the shrewdness behind it. When she answered she spoke with well feigned indifference:

"Well, Donny's a good kid and I hate to see anyone take it in the bankroll after he's gone this far. Besides the *Fads and Fancies* success means a C note for me every week it plays."

SHE WENT DOWN to the Amphion later and watched the chorus wreck a new routine Oscar Wren struggled with. He finally dismissed them for a duet rendered by the handsome juvenile and ingenue, and tipped a seat beside Lee.

"What's the use of all this struggle and strife," he mumbled, mopping his damp forehead, "when it's a nickel to a nosegay we won't open."

"Who says we won't?" Lee inquired.

"Donny. He's bogged down. He hasn't the chance of a cockroach in the hands of a child with a slipper. I'm even with the board but look what I've lost in time. The Chicago Civic wanted me to stage *'Butterfly'*."

"And Paramount wanted me to replace Burns and Allen," Lee drawled. "Don't be too sure about this show, Oscar. We might go through yet."

He looked at her swiftly. "You know—something?"

"If I did I wouldn't tell you," Lee responded amiably. "By the way, where's the boy impresario?"

"Downtown, trying to hock his insurance policy," the director explained. "Fancy that."

"You fancy it—I don't like it!" Lee answered.

At six that same night Lee dialed the same number she had called earlier in the day. She spoke with Sato and a minute later had Gluckman on the other end of the wire.

"That's a deal," she said, keeping her voice steady with an effort. "I'll be over Saturday with my trunk but—"

"Lee! Swell!"

"Wait. But first I've got to get the money. My boss needs it right off. I can't turn a wheel unless I'm oiled in advance."

"If I settle you won't take a powder?"

"Say," she said indignantly, "my word's my bond! I've never welched on a deal yet and I don't intend to start now!"

"Okay," Gluckman said soothingly, "forget I mentioned it. You'll get the money tomorrow. Remember, I won't be crude, either. I like unusual, odd things. Things that make a—ah—gift more attractive. And that reminds me. The shoes you were wearing at lunch seemed a bit worn—"

Again that night Donny took her home from the theatre. He was taciturn, gloomy and Lee knew he had something other than money on his mind.

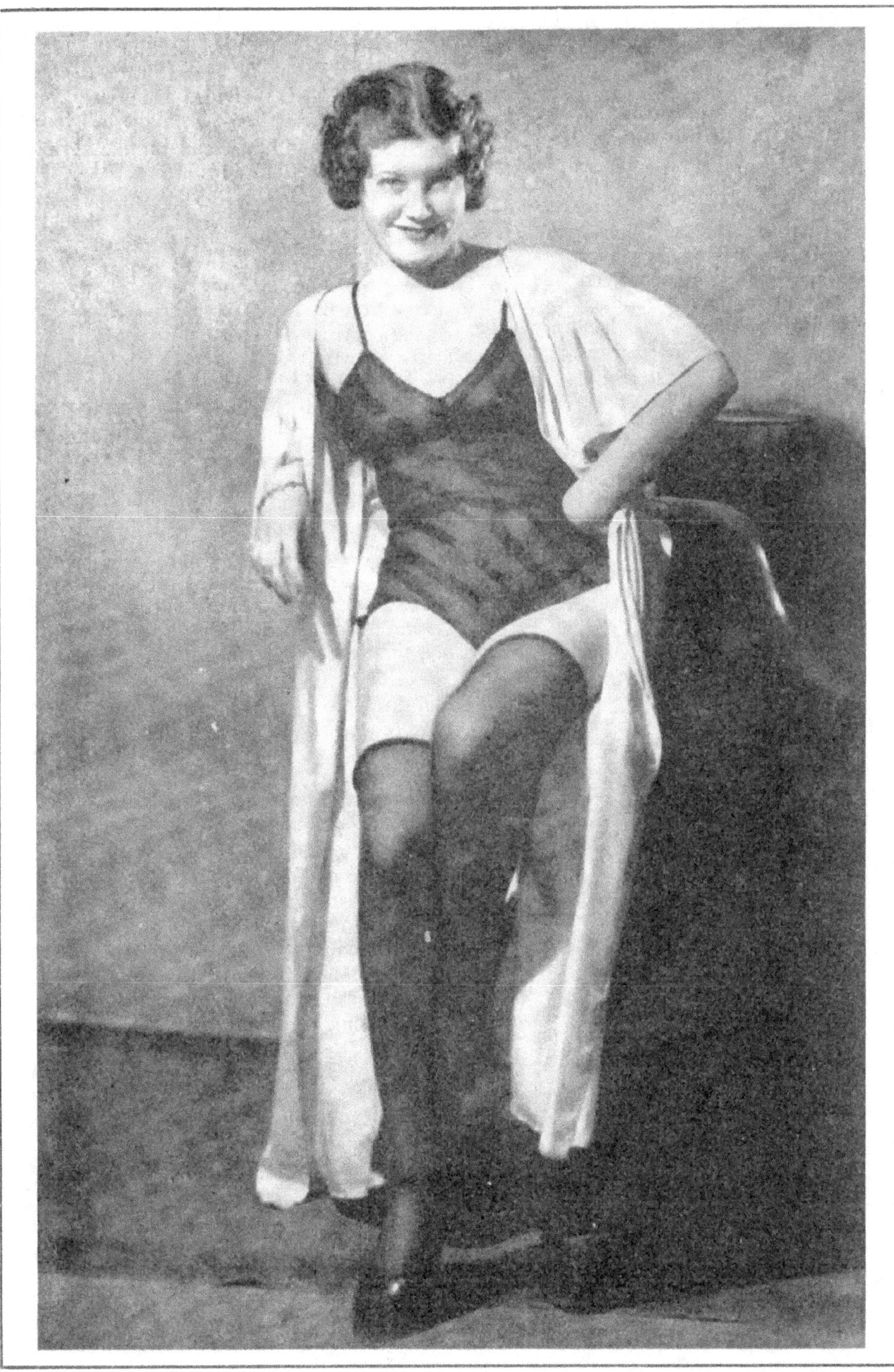

"What's the matter?" she asked, when they reached her apartment.

"You."

"What about—"

"Go ahead, get comfortable and I'll tell you."

LEE WENT IN HER bandbox bedroom and took off the dress she was wearing. She hung it up together with her slip. That left her in loose-legged pink panties and a net brassiere all too flimsy to entirely secure and hide completely the two mounds straining against it. She hid the svelte lines of her glamorous body in the folds of a corduroy dressing gown, shoved her small feet into puff-ball slippers and went back to the living room and the divan.

"Tell me," she requested, curling up beside him.

"I saw you coming out of the Dixie with Hy Gluckman," Donny began slowly. "I know what it means. You've been out trying to raise what I need. That's the story, isn't it?"

"Yes," Lee said faintly.

"At first I was sore," he went on in the same mechanical tone. "Then, I realized what a pal you're trying to be, and I felt sad. Listen. You love me, don't you?"

"Would I be here—close—like this, if I didn't?"

"And I'm crazy about you. Okay. You're my future happines, all I want, all I must have. Do you think I'm gonna toss all that away for a rotten five thousand dollars to sink in a musical piece, no matter how good I believe it is?"

"So what?" Lee whispered.

"I don't know what proposition you've made with Gluckman but no matter what it is, the first thing you do when you get up tomorrow morning—even before you clean your teeth and let the water run—you phone him and tell him it's all off—definitely and positively *off!* Understand?"

"Yes," Lee whispered. "Any—anything else?"

"Plenty!" Donny's voice grew vibrant. "Turn around, smile with parted lips and let me—" He took her in his arms.

She flexed herself to him, the same excited thrills shooting through her, while her breath came short and fast and her heart pounded.

"Oh, sweetheart," she cried softly, "I—I'd do *anything* for you—anything you wanted me to!"

LEE PHONED THE Gluckman pent-house as soon as she arose the next morning but Hy had left for his office. Then she put on the coffee pot, her thoughts divided between joy and grief, and only stirred when the bell buzzed.

A messenger boy stood on the threshold with a package under his arm.

"Miss Lee Brice?"

"I'm she. I mean, she's me. I should say I'm—"

"Sign here."

Lee took the package, shut the door and stripped off the paper wrappings. She removed the lid from the box and widened her eyes at the smart, modish pair of expensive shoes it contained. They were from the Rivoli on Fifth Avenue, they had high, delicately turned heels and Lee knew they never cost a cent under twenty-five or six dollars. Then, too, they were her size.

She lifted the right shoe out, felt the high heel turn, pivot-like in her hand and sat down to put it on. But the hell kept turning and—

AT TWO THAT afternoon an excited Lee got Oscar Wren aside and shoved five brand new one thousand dollar bills into his limp hand.

"Listen, pay attention!" she ordered sibilantly. "Here's the show's go-ahead, but you have to swear not to tell. You hand this jack to Donny. Tell him you won it last night on a full house or four aces. Tell him you inherited it—tell him anything, only don't mention *me* and be sure he gets it right away! Correct, got it?"

"Yes, ye gods!" the other choked.

After that Lee skipped away to telephone Gluckman again, got him finally, told him she wasn't playing ball on his team and rang off.

"That," she said happily, is *that!*"

Hy Gluckman, meanwhile almost broke his thumb dialing a number. "Rivoli Shoe Store?" he bawled, once he got the number. "This is Gluckman, Imperial Shoes, Park Avenue. Listen. I ordered a pair of Lady Aubrey specials sent up to Sixty-third Street, a Miss Brice. I want that order canceled immediately and the five thousand dollars in bills I left to be put in the removable heel of the right foot shoe sent back to me! Get it? Don't slip, do it right away!"

"Yes, Mr. Gluckman."

With a grunt he replaced the phone on its cradle and narrowed his small eyes. "The two-faced little heel!" he said, "I guess that will fix her!"

KILL OR CURE

By

CLAIRE KENNEDY

THE lush-bosomed chorine on Gil Rhodes' lap was engaged in a kissing marathon that slowly but surely was transferring most of her carmine lipstick to the young millionaire's mouth.

"You're such a honey," she cooed over and over again, thinking about the mink coat or diamond bracelet this little session would earn her.

Gil reached for his highball glass, found it empty. He rose suddenly, dumping the chorine on the floor. "Goin' home," he announced.

Despite the chorine's pleas and protestations, both physical and verbal, he got his hat and coat and made his way to the street. A taxi pulled up and engulfed him.

"Park Avenue," he mumbled. "Number 3500."

The cab ran along for a few blocks and then stopped. Gil leaned forward. "Whatsa matter?" he inquired.

"Red light, mister."

Gil Rhodes was drunk, but not drunk enough to ignore the figure of a beautiful blonde who had just stepped off the sidewalk into the glare of the taxi's headlights. His breath caught in his throat and he blinked to make certain the girl wasn't a figment of his Scotch-numbed mind.

She wasn't. She was flesh-and-blood. Delicious flesh-and-blood. Through a partial haze,Gil observed the cute, jiggling motion of her breasts as she crossed the street.

Now, that was something, he thought. Class from the tips of her toes to the chic chapeau on her golden head. Trim as a streamlined car. No chippy. No hot-blooded chorine with smeary red lips. Top flight.

He reached for the door handle. "Follow me," he said. "Keep following me."

Somehow Gil managed to stumble out of the taxi without falling. He started across the street after the beautiful blonde, weaving unsteadily on his pins.

THE GIRL HAD gone almost a full block before Gil caught up with her. He was almost at her side when he bumped into a fire hydrant and lost a good ten yards, not to mention gaining a barked knee. A second time he collided with a fat woman and almost knocked her over. Finally he was at her side. She swung along, head up and shoulders squared, her firm, jutting breasts punching out the lapels her tailored suit.

"You walk fast," Gil said.

She turned to look at him without slowing her pace. Her eyes were cobalt blue; steel ice behind curling lashes. Her head snapped front again.

"Too fast," Gil said. "Can't you slow up?"

The taxi was crawling along the curbing, keeping pace with them. The girl made no reply. Gil's inebriation was fast disappearing. He began to see things clearly and what he saw made him all the more anxious. He reached out and grabbed the girl's arm.

"Now, look—"

That was as far as he got. A tightly gloved hand struck him across the cheek with a report that sounded like a rifle shot. It wasn't any love pat, either. It was a solid crack that made Gil's head spin. When it stopped spinning, the blonde was gone.

"She ducked into that store, mister," the cab driver said, pointing to a sweet shop.

Gil touched his cheek gingerly. It smarted. He stumbled into the taxi. "She plays too hard. Take me home."

ARLENE RHODES GROUND her half-finished cigarette into an ash-tray. "I don't know what to do with him. He won't work, he won't take up sports, he won't do anything except drink and hang around night clubs. This is a prime example of how too much money can ruin someone."

Dr. Frank Miller smiled and placed an arm around Arlene's shoulder. "You mustn't fret about it, darling. He'll wake up."

"Yes, he does—at two o'clock every afternoon."

"I mean he'll come to his senses. After all,

you can't throw your life away worrying about him. Why not marry me and come away for a long honeymoon? You need the rest."

"And leave him behind? He'll drink himself to death. No, I can't do that, Frank. I promised Dad I'd see that he made something of himself. I've got to keep that promise." She bit her lips nervously. "If I could only get him interested in a girl or get a girl interested in him. Someone to pull him out of this rut. Someone to—"

Frank Miller swung her around. "Arlene! I've got just the girl! She'll either kill him or cure him!"

"Who is she?"

"She studied nursing. I met her at the hospital. I think she's looking for something now. But you've got to promise me one thing."

"Oh, there's a catch."

"Of course. I'm completely mercenary. You've got to promise that if I straighten out Gilbert you'll marry me."

She swayed into the young physician's arms. "Yes." Her lips brushed his. "It won't be as simple as you think it is."

"I'll take that chance. Everything must be done as I direct."

"All right."

Frank kissed her to seal the bargain.

It was Saturday night—almost a week later—when Arlene, Frank Miller and Gil were seated at a table at the expensive *Dream Club*.

Gil's eyes were beginning to glaze over. He lifted his highball glass to his lips. "So," he said for the fifth time, "you're getting married."

Frank smiled. "That's right, Gil. This is in the nature of an engagement party. Informal, of course. Another drink?"

Arlene pinched Frank's thigh under the table. "He's drunk now," she whispered.

"Sure," Gil said. "Same thing."

Frank motioned to a waiter. "One double Scotch," he said.

The double Scotch did the trick. Gil went out like a light, much to Arlene's embarrassed disgust. Frank and a waiter got him out to the physician's car and bundled him in.

"This seems like a strange method of curing him," Arlene snapped peevishly.

Frank started the car. "I said I'd kill *or* cure him. I'll take you home first."

"But what are you going to do with Gilbert?"

"Never mind. I have more at stake than he has. I'll take care of him."

Arlene shook her head. "I hope so."

Gil Rhodes always kept a bottle of Scotch in the drawer of the night table beside his bed. When he awoke with a hangover—which was seven mornings or afternons out of seven—he reached for the bottle automatically and downed a slug of straight whiskey.

But this time there was no night table, no drawer and no bottle of Scotch when he cracked his heavy-lidded eyes. He groped for a moment or two, staring up at the strange, unfamiliar ceiling. It seemed to be sloping. Or maybe he was sloping.

"Jenkins!" he called. "Jenkins, where are you?"

There was no answer. Gil sat up, rubbed his aching head. To all appearances, although it was ridiculous, he had been sleeping on a cot in a log cabin.

"Jenkins! Jenkins!" His voice echoed through the wooded section around the cabin, came back at him mockingly. Gil swung his legs off the cot and indulged in a little more puzzled head rubbing.

"Did you call?" a voice queried.

Gil looked up, startled. He was more startled when he saw the girl standing in the doorway, her arms loaded with split wood. He shook his head, certain that if he cleared it the girl would vanish. She didn't. She came closer, leaned over and dropped the wood into a box. She was wearing the most abbreviated bathing suit Gil had ever seen—and he had seen some super-abbreviated bathing suits.

Actually, it wasn't a bathing suit at all. A narrow strip of printed cotton covered and cupped the high, perking hills of her breasts. Tight shirring pinched the strip together in the deep valley between the twin charms. Shorts of the same material molded the most beautifully arched hips this side of Venus di Milo. Her thighs, round and plump, were tanned a warm shade of brown.

Once he had temporarily finished taking an inventory of her bodily charms, Gil gazed at her face. That gave him the shock of his life. She was the beautiful blonde he had tried to pick up that night the taxi followed him! She was the blonde who had slapped his face! He couldn't be mistaken. There was no doubt about it. And yet, she didn't seem to recognize him.

"You were calling for someone," she said. Her voice was deep and throaty. It sent funny little sensations racing up and down Gil's spine. "Someone named Jenkins."

"My—my valet," Gil said.

She posed with her hands on the lyre of her hips, a faintly disdainful smile curling her plump, red lips. "I rather thought you'd have one of those things. You're the type. How about some coffee? You could probably stand a gallon."

She grinned. "That's too many questions at once." She stepped to a closet, removed a pair of knitted swimming trunks. "You can use these if you can get 'em on. I'll be down at the brook."

SHE WAS GONE BEFORE Gil could protest. He sat there, holding the trunks she had tossed into his lap and wondering how all this had happened. He remembered going out with Arlene and Frank Miller. He remembered that

Frank and Arelne were going to get married. After that he remembred nothing.

How in the name of heaven he had ever gotten to this log cabin was a mystery. How the same blonde who had slapped him had gotten there was a double mystery.

He was a little amazed to find himself shedding his trousers and donning the slightly small swimming trunks. It had been five years since he had even thought about swimming in anything but Scotch.

And yet, here he was, Gil Rhodes, New York's man-about-a-bottle, picking his way

"Got a drink?" Gil blurted out quickly.

She stepped to a pump, raised the handle. "Clear, fresh and cold. Right out of the well."

Gil made a wry face. "Ugh! Not water!"

She shrugged. "Sorry, I'm all out of champagne. Water won't poison you, Mr. Rhodes."

Gil's brows arched. "How do you know my name?"

"Found a card in your pocket. I'd suggest a short swim in the brook. Best thing in the world for a hangover."

"Say, listen, how did I get here, where am I and who are you?"

down to the crystal clear pool of a mountain brook. When he reached the bank he saw the luscious blonde floating on the surface of the placid, transparent water, the coned hills of her breasts punching up like miniature buoys.

"Come on in," she called. "It's swell!"

Gil tested the water with his big toe. A cold chill ran up his spine. It was like sticking his foot in a bowl of ice cubes.

"F-freezing," he stuttered.

She swam close to the bank. The refraction of the clear water made her gorgeous bosom seem larger and more voluptuous. Gil was looking at it. He didn't see her hand shoot out and grab his ankle.

THE NEXT MOMENT he hit the water stomach first. He went down and came up, spluttering like a porpoise. "It's like ice!" he cried. "I'm freezing!"

She climbed up on the bank, water dripping from her bare, dimpled stomach; the wet cotton bandeau revealing the mature fullness of her flint-peaked breasts.

"Good for you," she said. "There'll be coffee and pancakes at the cabin when you get out."

"I—I'm getting out r-right n-now!" Gil paddled to the bank and hauled his frigid body out of the water. He was gasping and half-frozen.

The blonde smiled down at him. "Too bad Jenkins isn't here to warm your tootsies."

Gil got to his feet. "Now, listen, young lady," he began. It was as far as he got. She started towards the cabin.

"Make it snappy," she said. "I'll have breakfast in five minutes."

At the cabin she gave him an old pair of trousers and a woodsman's shirt, sent him outside to dress. Gil tried to grumble but he didn't feel the least bit like grumbling. In fact, he felt swell—and hungry. The pungent, tantalizing odor of percolating coffee made him almost ravenous.

WHEN HE STEPPED INTO the cabin, she was making pancakes at the wood stove. She had changed into culottes and a turtle-neck sweater. The latter, tight across her jutting, tilted breasts, couldn't have been more revealing.

Gil came up behind her and placed his hands on her hips. "What's your name?"

"Hands off the cook," she said.

Gil kept his hands where they were. He could feel the heat of her body through the cotton culottes. "What's your name?"

"What's the difference?" Deftly, she loaded a plate with golden-brown cakes. "Here, start on those."

A half hour later, Gil pushed back from the table. "Gee," he said. "I had twenty-three cakes and two cups of coffee."

The blonde smiled. "And no liquor."

"I could use a drink."

She motioned to the pump. "Clear, cold and refreshing."

"Forget it. Do I get my questions answered? How, where and why?"

"How, where and why what?"

"How did I get here, where am I and why?"

She leaned back in her chair. "Well, about midnight a car stopped on the main road. It made a racket and woke me up. I went out to see what happened. They had a flat. Two men and a girl. You were one of the men. They stretched you out on the grass while they fixed the flat. Then they drove off, forgetting all about you. I dragged you into the cabin. That's all."

IT SOUNDED LOGICAL. Two men and a girl meant Frank Arlene and himself. "But where am I?"

"About forty miles from the city. This is my cabin. I'm spending a week here."

"What's your name?"

She started to clear the table. "Betty Larson. Does that mean anything to you?"

Gil helped her with the dishes. He was dying to tell her about the incident on the street but he restrained himself. It certainly was a small world.

The dishes done, she turned to Gil. "I suppose you'll be wanting to get back to the city."

"Don't suppose so much."

She shrugged. "I'm going for a walk."

"So am I," Gil said.

They were deep in the woods when Gil made the first break. "I like you," he said.

She didnt' answer for a long time. Then: "Thanks."

They found a cleared space and sat down. Betty stretched out with one arm under her head and her breasts raised alluringly. Gil's eyes drank in the lithe loveliness of her figure.

"I like you a lot," he said, moving closer to her.

Her eyes flickered. "What do you want me to say?"

"That you like me."

"But I don't."

"Why not?"

"Mind if I look over your shoulder while you work?"

She looked away. "I don't care for human sponges."

"I could stop drinking."

"Could you?"

"If I had something to substitute for it." He reached out and dropped his hand on the curve above her hip. "Something like you."

She moved away. "None of that, please."

"Betty." There was a throb in Gil's voice. "This is on the level." His arm snapped around her waist, drew her close against him. "You're the first girl I ever—"

SHE BRACED THE palms of her hands against his chest. "Tried to pick up on the street?"

"Then you knew me!" Gil gasped.

"Of course. Let me go."

"Oh, no. I'm sober now and I'm going to stay sober."

"For how long?"

"Forever, if—"

"Oh, there's a catch."

"You're the catch. I'll stay sober if you—if you—" Emotion got the best of Gil. He placed one hand at the back of her head and forced her soft lips against his mouth. She struggled to release herself but Gil held her in a tight embrace.

When he finally drew his mouth away she was panting and her cheeks were rose red. "You can slap the other cheek now," Gil said.

She scrambled to her feet. "Let's go back to the cabin. This is—this is—"

Gil came up next to her and imprisoned her in his arms. "This is wonderful, darling!" he cried, joining his mouth to her lips again.

She didn't fight against him any more. Her body was limp and relaxed. Slowly, her arms encircled his neck. The soft warmth of her against him quickened the beat of his heart and sent the blood rushing up to his head. He dropped one hand to the curve of her hip and followed an undulating line that led to the hollow beneath her shoulder.

"You like me, don't you, Betty?" he whispered, once their mouths were apart.

THE RAUCOUS TOOT of an automobile horn came faintly from the road. Betty stiffened "It's your friends," she panted. "They've come for you."

Gil's hands caressed her body. "They can wait. You like me, don't you?"

"Sober, yes."

"I'll always be sober."

The horn blew insistently. "We'd better go back," Betty said.

Gil held her close. "Before we do you've got to promise me something."

"What?"

"That you'll marry me."

"Oh, but—"

"There aren't any buts. Either you marry me or I'll drink myself to death."

She smiled. "That's funny. I was supposed to kill or cure you."

"What do you mean?"

"Never mind. I think I'd rather cure you."

Gil's brow wrinkled. "You're talking in riddles. Will you marry me?"

She clung to him. "Yes."

Gil turned his cheek. "Slap me, darling! I want to make sure I'm awake!"

Betty tapped him lightly. "You're awake."

He squeezed her. "That was a lot different from the first slap."

She raised her kissable lips. "You're a lot different, too."

Gil kissed her fervently.

MY MAN

A dillar, a dollar, a ten o'clock scholar,
And nobody thinks he's bright;
He may not be smart in the daytime
But he's terribly clever at night!

BIG BOY

A COLD, cutting wind swept down Prescott Street. It carried a knife in its teeth and made a pass at Jan Shaw as she flew up the steps of her boarding house. She unlocked the front door with shivering fingers and became a study in suspended motion as Mrs. Lennigan, her landlady, glided out of the front parlor.

Mrs. Lennigan had two sharp eyes and three good teeth. She displayed them in a grim smile as she reached out and took the latch key from Jan's gloveless fingers.

"I'm sorry, Miss Shaw, but I've rented your room. I'm holding your trunk until you pay the three weeks you owe me. I warned you Thursday—no rent—out!"

Jan's big brown eyes fixed wonderingly on the leathery face of the woman confronting her. She didn't know what to do. "Out" sounded too much like cheap melodrama and still—

"But where can I go?" she asked unsteadily. "I know I'll get that model's job next week and if you can wait—"

Mrs. Lennigan interrupted by opening the front door. She dodged the gust of icy wind that blew in and turned to Jan.

"Good night, Miss Shaw, and good luck. Remember you can have your trunk whenever you pay up. I'm within my legal rights as any lawyer will tell you."

Ten minutes later Jan turned into the cafeteria at Willow and Benson Avenues. It was warm and steamy. She fingered the solitary quarter in her purse as Kitty, the new waitress, loomed up beside her.

" 'Lo, Jan. Tough night, ain't it? What can I get you?"

"A furnished room," Jan smiled thinly. "I have just been ousted from mine!"

Kitty toyed with her starched apron strings. "I can do better than that," she said confidentially. "I can get you a whole private house—all for yourself. Look." She leaned over. "I was Miss Sandra Athling's maid until she left

"That scenery you're hanging on to. Are you gonna drop it or—"

Blue

By W. Archer Sayers

"Don't you dare lay a finger on me! I—I'll scream!"

for Europe and threw me out on my ear, the hussy! Do you think I'd be slaving here if it wasn't for that dame? Not a chance!"

Jan relaxed, her brown eyes intent on Kitty's pretty Irish face. "But about the whole house—"

"I've still got the front door key to the Athling's place! I never turned it in! Here! She fumbled in the pocket of the skirt under the apron and an instant later Jan's fingers tightened about the thin shank of another key. "This opens the works. They've got an oil burner left on to keep the pipes from freezing and all you gotta do is flip the switch in the hall. Go ahead—make yourself comfortable—she won't be back until April."

"But—if—if—"

"Ham and eggs, did you say?" Kitty cut in loudly. "Coming right up. 'Sweethearts forever with French frys'," she called in the direction of the kitchen. Then, swiftly, to Jan: "Don't be an utnay, honey. Nothing's going to happen to you and—it's two below outside by our best thermometer."

AS SHE BUCKED THE wind that blew her toward aristocratic Congress Boulevard, Jan remembered what she had read about Sandra Athling. The gal was high society. The Athling family was in Florida but Sandra had elected to stay home—that is, until, as Kitty explained, at the last moment she had heard some rich playboy she was fond of, had booked passage on a France bound liner.

Without warning then, Sandra Athling had hurled a pair of panties and a fresh brassiere in a wardrobe trunk and kicked out to follow. Jan glowed inwardly as she reached her destination and scuttled up the brown stone front steps like a frightened rabbit. . .

What a break! The key fit the door and the knob turned without difficulty. The next minute she was in an awesome foyer where oil paintings stared down at her, flipping the heat switch as directed and listening to the thump of her heart. Cautiously, her steps muffled by the thick carpet, Jan ascended a spiral staircase and found Miss Athling's suite on the second floor.

The heat had come on more fully and it was now comfortable. She kindled a pair of boudoir lamps and gasped at the luxury surrounding her. The boudoir was done in mauve and silver, the bedroom in pearl gray and green. And the inviting bath in black and gold. Jan took off her hat and coat and peered around with wide, interested eyes.

She began to feel more at ease. The heat got into her bones and thawed her out. After she had opened the wardrobe closets and eyed the loveliness of the gowns hanging in silent rows, Jan decided to take a shower and turn in. It had been a tough day, tramping from agency to agency, in search of a job and the Lennigan episode had topped it fittingly.

She undressed slowly, hanging her shabby skirt, her worn coat and her rayon blouse in the closet. She rolled her much-used girdle and stuck it on a shelf. Her stockings and shoes went under a *chaise-longue* and Jan went into the adjoining bath.

She couldn't resist a peek at herself in a full length cheval mirror. She stood still, gazing at her naked charms with shadowed eyes. A body like hers and she couldn't get a position as a model anywhere! She looked at the suave, sweet, flowing lines of her form. At the the two firm, uplifted breasts that maturely swelled from her round, white domes. She took in the details of her torso, the flat tummy with its dimple, the waist, so slender, the thighs so seductive and the legs symmetrical and shapely.

WATER CASCADED OVER her in a brilliant rain. Jan exulted in the brisk shower, the warmth of the heated towels she rubbed herself briskly with, the quilted French lounging robe she borrowed from the boudoir. Her feet encased themselves in a smart little morocco slippers and a cigarette completed the languor inspired by the rich comfort of her bath.

It was when she was busy selecting a nightie that she first heard it. The bell rang first. That was followed by a pulse-chilling staccato rapping on the lower front door. Jan's vivid lips parted in dismay.

She had to do something! She couldn't sit there and let whoever it was batter down the door. Hugging the robe to her she hurried down the spiral stairs and opened the door.

Jan suppressed a gasp of alarm as she saw her visitor. A good looking traffic cop in a blue uniform, his lean face red with the cold, walked in! He shut the door and let his gaze rove over Jan.

"So," he said, taking off leather gloves and moving his fingers forward and back.

"So—what?"

"Who are you?" he asked.

"Me?" Jan smiled. "I'm Sandra—Miss Athling, why?"

His bright blue eyes narrowed slightly. He was terribly attractive, Jan decided, so virile and big and handsome. She couldn't remember having seen him on duty anywhere before and that was her loss.

"I was going off duty, on my way home," he explained, "when I saw the light upstairs. I thought Miss Athling—you—were away."

"I was," Jan said demurely, "but I came back. People do, you know."

He nodded. "Sure. My mistake. Sorry. By the way, you haven't a—a nip handy, have you? It's a bit chilly out."

"Come upstairs. I—I had the wine closet locked when I left but I'll see what I can do." Jan, as she led the way to the floor above and the small study at its head, was amazed at her own ease. She was really enjoying the situation. It was the first time she had doubled for a society deb and she was doing well for herself. "By the way," she asked, "what did you say your name was, officer?"

"I didn't," he grinned, "but it's Foster, Bill Foster of the Eighth Precinct Traffic. I got the Congress and North Street beat."

"Sit here, take your coat off, make yourself comfortable," Jan invited, "and I'll be back in a jiffy."

AS LUCK HAD IT she found a quart of Scotch, some glasses and a bottle of carbonated water in the dining room buffet. When she went back to the study Bill Foster was sprawled out in a large leather chair, a cigar clamped between his white teeth. Jan secretly thrilled to his size and clean cut bulk. Not only that, she felt, but there was something about him that appealed to her—some charm of personality—that impressed itself on her.

She poured out two drinks. It was fine old Scotch, mellow, smooth and with a peat tang that warmed her pleasantly. Jan took her glass and curled up on the end of a small sofa. She could see his glance moving over her and for the first time she realized how scantily clad she was.

It might have been the liquor or the excitement of outwitting the law, but a wave of reckless daring rolled over Jan. All at once she found herself wanting to be as alluring as possible—to weave a subtle feminine spell of beauty and seduction about him—to arouse his interest and hold it. His very presence was inspiring to her heated fancies.

Bill flushed slightly and grinned. Jan bit her full nether lip. Why on earth had she said *that?* He'd think she was trying to make him or something—that she was just another bored, rich girl, with a yen to play around with any strong, handsome stranger.

All at once, she found she wanted to be as alluring as possible.

"Where've you been, Miss Athling?"

It was on the tip of Jan's red tongue to say Europe. "B-Bermuda," she managed to get out in time.

He nodded again and looked at the bottle. He grinned broadly as he tilted it. "Best Scotch I ever drank. How about Peter Barclay, Miss Athling?"

Jan took a stab in the dark and hit the bull's eye. "You mean my boy friend?" When Bill inclined his head, she laughed. "Oh, he's out—definitely."

"You'll make up."

"Not this time, John Copper." She was feeling flippant. "It's on, it's off and it's off for good. I'm foot loose and fancy free and I—I do admire large gentlemen in blue suits."

She sank further back among the sofa's cushions. Her pose was one of sensuous enchantment. So Cleopatra might have arranged her fascinating figure the night Mark Anthony had a date on the well known Love Barge. Lights glimmered along Jan's ivory legs as far as her dimpled knees. The robe slipped from one alabaster shoulder leaving it bare and beguiling. Her crimson mouth quivered and her large breasts pushed out the front of the gown as her breathing quickened.

All at once she saw something about her amorous posture had captivated her visitor. Bill's blue eyes began to spark. His hand was not entirely steady as he picked up his glass and took a long drink. It was so quiet she could hear his noisely swallow.

"Guess I'l be going," he mumbled, a trifle thickly ."Glad everything's okay here. Gotta be careful. There's a lug on the loose called Barney Harlow who makes a specialty of private houses. He's a roof prowler and pops around when least expected. Thanks for the red-eye."

"Do you have—to go?" Jan's soft lips curved. "I mean, have you got a wife and kiddies—"

"Not me! I'm a bachelor, I am. But, yes," he gave her an uneasy look. Jan didn't know it but the robe had slid further up one of the shapely legs. Beyond the knee, it let a portion of her rounded thigh spring into view, while it bulged at the waist, disclosing hidden curves of warm delight and pink flesh. "Yes," he added, still thickly, "I know I got to scram!"

"It was sweet of you to stop."

She was busy selecting a nightie—and then she heard it—a pulse-chilling rapping on the door!

"Don't get up, Miss Athling. I'll get out okay." He shifted his weight from one foot to the other. "Er—mind if I tell you something? You—you're the prettiest gal I've ever seen anywhere—"

He was gone before Jan fully interpreted the statement. She heard the lower door slam shut and the heavy beat of her pulses. A delicious tide of tingling pleasure swept through her blood. So he didn't think she was a fresh society punk on the make? He did like her or he wouldn't have said what he did!

For a long, blissful interval Jan reclined on the couch thinking about him. What blue eyes he had! What a personality and what masculine appeal! Why hadn't he stayed? Perhaps, she told herself, she should be glad he hadn't.

By degrees Jan became conscious of a cool current of air seeping in through the study door. It stopped after a time, but she drew her delicately arched brows together as she heard a door close with eerie abruptness. She was half erect on the sofa when a quick shadow fell across the rug and a vice said:

"Not a chirp, sweetheart, and you won't get hurt!"

Jan almost fainted as a slim, small, dark-faced youth in frayed trousers, sweater and cap slid into the room. He carried a short-nosed automatic in one hand and his eyes, she saw, were deep-set and sharp.

Before Jan could speak or move he caught sight of the Scotch, grabbed the bottle up and, scorning a glass, put it to his twisted lips and took a long satisfying swig.

"Baby, what fire-water!" He turned to the sofa, shoving the gun in under the sweater. His eyes brightened as they fell more completely on her. "I've had this dump on my list for a long time. Been away? I should have stopped in before now—or mebbe I didn't make no mistake waiting! Get up!"

"Get—"

"Up!" he rapped out. "I want to take a look at you. It's so long since I've seen a sweet face with swell daisy-stems that I got a yen—What are you wearing under that robe, sweetheart?"

"None of your business!" Jan snapped.

"Oh, tough gal? Listen, sister, don't get hard with me because that's my racket, see? A grand looker like you shouldn't talk back, never. Just for curiosity I'll take a look. C'mon, shed, moult!"

Jan's brown eyes widened indignantly. "I—I just took a bath and I'm not clothed—underneath!"

"Ain't that nice?" A muscle twitched in his weathered face. "How do you know I believe you? You'd better lemme see for myself—"

Jan hugged the French robe tighter to her curved figure. "I'll do nothing of the kind! What do you think this is—a burlesque show?"

"Yeah, a private one of my own! Just a little look, a couple of kisses, some silverware and jewelry and I'll be on my way? Fair enough, eh? Let it flutter, baby!"

He took a step toward her. He was beginning to breathe hard and Jan didn't like the signs flaring in his unshaven face. She thought fast! First the law, then the underworld! She was on a spot, in a jam! A cold shiver ran the length of her spine. She asked herself desperately how she could stall him off.

"Look. The silver's downstairs in the buffet. You take it and scram and I won't say a word—"

"Later. Don't worry, I'll clean from roof to cellar. First, that scenery you're hanging onto. Are you gonna drop it or—"

"*No!*"

"Then I'll give you a hand—"

"Stand back! Don't you dare to lay a finger on me! I—I'll scream!"

His lips curled back over broken teeth. He gave her a mocking grin. "Gonna scream? Ain't that nice. Wanna get your neck all black-and-blued, huh? Okay, babe. Just for that—"

Jan did scream when he reached her. She ducked nimbly, his hands stretched out to clasp her and collided with the end of the sofa. Jan lost her balance and fell. Her head struck the arm of the sofa and, as quickly as if the moon and stars had been turned off, all went black!

Minutes, hours or years later she opened her eyes. The taste of Scotch tingled in her mouth and throat. Her head ached dully, but she forgot all about that when she found she was stretched out on the sofa and that someone leaned over, arranging the quilted robe.

Jan looked up and into a pair of smiling blue eyes.

"Bill!" she cried faintly.

"In person." The hand on her arm trembled oddly. "Everything's okay, take it easy. I shut

(*Please turn to page* 60)

HERE'S HOW!

By

ANN LAWRENCE

"What did you do to me? Where are you taking me?"

"ALL right," Betty said, "if you recommend this drink I guess it's all right." There was no indication in her tone of voice that only a half hour before she had overheard her escort Stan, plotting to get her plastered.

"A boilermaker's what you need," Stan insisted, "but I can't say I think much of your choice of places. This is a regular dive."

Betty leaned against the sloppy bar and looked around complacently, while Stan gave the order. She'd picked out the worst looking place she could see when Stan, in keeping with the plan she'd overheard had suggested a drink before they went to the house where they were to change into the costumes for the fancy dress ball at the Yacht Club.

She was a bit disappointed with the customers. She'd hoped for gangsters and thugs, and apparently everyone there were honest working men. Like the huge, broad shouldered man in well worn overalls standing next to them against the sloppy bar.

The bartender put down the two boilermakers. Stan raised his small glass. "Here's how," he said.

The man in overalls turned around and scowled at them. He didn't say anything until Betty had drained the last of her beer chaser. Then Stan ordered another round.

"That's no drink for a lady," the man in overalls snarled.

Betty laughed at him. "Who says I'm a lady?" she wanted to know.

"You'd better," Stan said, "mind your own business, fellow."

The bartender put down the second round. Stan tossed his off. Betty reached for hers. The man in overalls spilled the contents of the smaller glass onto the bar. He tossed down some silver. "Better give her a lemonade," he said to the bartender.

Stan had the courage of two boilermakers under his belt. He pushed Betty to one side. "Listen," he began.

The man in overalls put a mammoth hand on Stan's chest. "I don't want to listen," he snapped.

Stan made a big mistake. He started a swing toward a massive jaw.

Betty could have sworn the big man's fist didn't travel more than six inches, but Stan seemed to jump up in the air, before landing on the back of his neck in the sawdust.

That was about the last clear sight Betty had for some time. There was a confused picture of the bartender starting to climb over the bar. There were loud whoops as other customers turned in to take a hand in an obviously welcome fight. The bartender led with his chin and was draped back onto a pile of his own glasses. Tables overturned, a chair splintered over a head and shoulders. Steely fingers closed around her arm and she was jerked sidewise with a suddenness that nearly snapped her neck.

She let out only one yell before she found herself being pulled through a back door into an evil smelling alley. It was just near enough to dark to make things indistinct.

The big man pulled her swiftly along, turned into a darker side opening and crouched with her behind a row of garbage cans. He kept his hand over her mouth until footsteps pounded past. A siren started screaming, coming closer and closer.

Betty heard a muttered curse and then she was picked up. But never for an instant during the moments that followed did that hand leave her lips. Then something crashed into her head. A burst of fire seemed to split her skull, and blankness descended.

Betty came back to a gradual consciousness. She was aware of a continual joggling and jolting, and of flashes of passing light that hurt her eyes when she opened them. She was propped up in the corner of a coupe, and the red headed man was driving. Her sidewise look showed her the strong jaw in profile against a passing street light.

She started to say, "Where am I?" when she suddenly realized that someone had done things to her blouse. It was still opened far below the top. Even in the light of the dash, Betty could see the motion produced by the joggling of the car. And what was worse, the blouse was wet where it *did* cover her!

She reached up cautious fingers and started buttoning her blouse, imprisoning again the half visible truants.

The man said, "So you're back with us again!"

"You don't sound very happy about it," Betty complained. "And what did you do to me? Where're you taking me? And what happened?"

"I'm not happy! I didn't do anything to you. You clunked your head on a post we were passing. Then you fainted. The doc told me nothing much was wrong with you so I started riding you around till you snapped out of it. You sure got me in a swell jam!"

"I got *you* in a jam!" Betty said. "That's fine coming from you. You started things at the bar—but by the way what's your name?"

The man slowed the car down. He turned and glowered at her. "My name's Percy," he snapped, "and I'm a boilermaker by trade. You think that's funny, or want to make something out of it?"

Betty cut off her laugh in the middle. "N-no," she managed. "But why'd you say I got you in a jam?"

"I rescued you, see, from that punk who was trying to get you drunk. Did you know that?"

"Yes," Betty admitted, "I overheard him planning it with one of his friends. He was doing it because he said I was such a stick."

"So you were going to show him you weren't—eh? All right, now listen a minute."

Percy snapped on the radio and turned to the police band.

"Calling all cars—calling all cars. Be on the look-out for Betty Anson, daughter of millionaire banker, believed kidnaped by man answering to following description—" There followed a fairly good tally of Percy's frame and features and clothing.

PERCY SNAPPED OFF the radio. "Your boy friend's work! I had to drive you around until you woke up. Them coppers might have let me have it first and talked about it later if they'd seen you with me."

"Yeah. And you don't need to get snooty about it. You're not any different than other dames." Another passing light showed his grin as he turned toward her, "Only nicer," he added.

"You talk like you'd had a lot of experience," Betty managed at last.

"Even a boilermaker gets around," Percy said.

He started a swing toward a massive jaw!

"But the doctor?" she inquired.

"Aw—he's a right guy. He won't split."

Betty thought fast. She figured a man who "split" on such a thing as kidnaping, wasn't quite so innocent as an honest boilermaker.

"I get it," she said aloud. She added, "Say, who pulled me all apart?"

She could have sworn that Percy blushed. Either that or the light they passed just then had a reddish glass.

Percy said, "I thought you'd knocked yourself off. I had to see if your heart was going."

Betty thought about that. Suddenly she was very conscious of her thumping heart. "I trust it was going?" she said sarcastically.

"O.K. Percy. We'll admit you're hot stuff. But how about letting me go now?"

"Glad to," Percy said. He stopped the coupe with what Betty considered unnecessary celerity.

"You sound like you'd be glad to get rid of me," she complained.

"I would," Percy said, "I thought you were just a nice kid in a jam when I went to bat for you back in the bar. Now—well I guess you're just like the rest of the stuffed shirts. Anything for a kick. And that reminds me. I might give you a real one—as you get out!" He lifted a heavy foot from the pedal.

BETTY STOPPED THE process of climbing out. She had the door open but that was as far as it went. She wondered if she could slide out backward—to protect herself—to be sure he wouldn't do anything behind her back.

"Well, what're you waiting for?" Percy demanded.

"I—I was just thinking about what you said. About my friends, I mean," she added quickly because she didn't want to bring up the subject of kicking again, "you're really wrong about them. Some of them're swell people."

"Nuts," said Percy.

Betty decided to stick to her guns. "You can say that, but you don't know. You've never really met them. Socially, I mean."

Percy grinned. "O.K., then babe. Suppose you and I trot up to your Dad's house and meet a bunch. I bet they'd sure be glad to see me. Yeah. You know how!"

Betty knew there was truth in his words. She could imagine the face of Juggins, their butler if such a thing should happen.

Percy seemed to read her silence correctly. "Tell you what," he suggested, "if you're game, I'll take you to a real blowout. Where you can have a swell time and meet some regular guys."

"Like your doctor friend, no doubt?" Betty suggested sarcastically.

Percy said, "Yeah, maybe you can even meet the croaker. How about it—or are you satisfied with just seeing how one half lives?"

Betty hesitated only a few seconds. "You're on, Percy. I guess I'll be safe enough with you."

Percy didn't seem to like that much. He said, "Depends on you, Babe," and then started staring at her.

Betty fidgeted. "Well, what's wrong? Am I coming apart or losing something again?"

"No. I was just thinking. You can't go in those clothes though."

"What's wrong with my clothes?" Betty demanded, "they're even getting dry from where you dumped water all over me."

"Tell you what's wrong with them!" he snapped. "I'm not going to have my friends think I'm dragging a rich dame around. No, babe, if you go with me you gotta dress like everybody else. But I know a guy where we can get some right clothes."

HE STARTED THE MOTOR and got the car under way just as a police car screamed past them, turning a searchlight into the coupe. Percy swore and trod on the accelerator. Brakes of the police car squealed. It started to turn around. Percy swung around a corner, took an alley corner on two wheels, cut through a parking lot and then really settled down to drive.

They played tag with two other police cars before Percy stopped the coupe in a dark side street. "Come on babe," he snapped.

Betty "came on" simply because she couldn't do anything else. Not when he had his huge paw wrapped around her arm and was pulling her.

They darted into a dark doorway of a pawn shop. Percy did things with a bell. It wasn't long before the door opened a crack. Far enough so Percy reached inside and grabbed a frightened little man. "Don't make a peep," he said, "you know me but keep names outa this."

Percy pushed the little man further in and pulled Betty inside. There was light enough for her to see Percy's command for the pawnbroker to keep still was useless. The man couldn't talk. Not when Percy had hold of his face!

She saw the look of fear leave the pawnbroker's face and knew that he'd recognized Percy. The big redhead removed his muzzling hand.

"What you want?" the little man asked.

"Clothes for babe here," Percy said.

"O.K. Come this way."

Betty soon discovered that Percy had violent likes and dislikes in the matter of clothes he thought fitting. After making one or two suggestions she kept still and let him pick out what he wanted. She wasn't a bit thrilled at the tight waisted plaid skirt, the red beret, or the sleasy sweater he picked out. She knew enough to keep that to herself, though.

"All right," Percy said when she took the bundle, "put 'em on!"

"Here?" she gasped.

"Sure. Unless you want to change in the car. And I don't think the cops'd give you much chance. They're probably all looking for the coupe now."

"But I can't change right here," Betty wailed.

"Oh. I see. Beat it Moe," Percy said. The pawnbroker grinned and left.

"You're still here," Betty pointed out.

her milky skin which lent warmth to the sheer step-ins she wore.

SHE WAS JUST STARTING to slip the skirt over her head when she realized Percy was watching her. He hadn't turned around, but he was staring directly into a mirror!

She was just slipping her skirt on when she realized Percy was watching her!

"Yeah. And that's not the last chapter. I'm going to stay here. You're not going to have a chance to go back now. I'll turn my back though."

Betty was able to recognize decision when she heard it. She waited until Percy had turned his broad back and slipped out of her clothes. Even the dim light made the most of

"Ohhhhh!" Betty gasped. She stood there motionless, her uplifted arms still holding the skirt, above her head.

Percy moved then, more quickly than even Betty would have guessed possible. She suddenly found herself engulfed in his arms. She tried to pull the skirt down, and succeeded in slipping it over Percy's head too. Principally because his lips were fastened to hers!

Betty started by burning with anger. Then

(*Please turn to page* 61)

That Certain Feeling

By

JACK ARNOLD

OLLY TRENT looked across the bridge table and sighed. She had just trumped her partner's ace, and the crime was doubly tragic inasmuch as her partner happened to be her husband.

"Sorry, dear," she murmured and flung him a worried glance. He pretended to smile, but she could see the little lines around his mouth tighten, and his eyes glare at her. To her right was seated Evelyn Cornish. Polly stole a glance at her now.

"I hate bridge," she wailed to Evelyn some time later when they were in the dressing room. "The cards all look alike except that I know some are pink and some are black. And Jim takes it so darned seriously. It's awful." She sighed deeply.

Evelyn made sympathetic noises with her tongue against her teeth. "It isn't sufficiently important to worry about," she told Polly comfortingly. "He'll forget it."

But Jim's voice cutting through the conversation was brusque.

"For heaven's sake, Polly, make it snappy, will you?"

"I must rush!" Polly grabbed her gloves and bag and rushed out to meet her impatient husband.

Evelyn turned back to the mirror, her eyes grave, her mouth trying not to curve into an indulgent smile. She knew both Polly and Jim well enough to recognize certain unmistakable signs of a pleasant enough marriage-bark drifting with unerring consistency towards some hidden shoals and blackish rocks.

Jim was one of those big, efficient, active people who invariably do everything right. His bridge was good, his golf excellent, his tennis better than average and his business —ah, Evelyn's pretty lips puckered up into a thoughtful whistle.

For of all things, Jim manufactured candy bars! Very good candy bars, too—and a wide seller, as Evelyn had occasion to know. For Evelyn had the account nicely tied up, it being the one account which kept her advertising agency out of the red.

Of course, more recently Jim had shown a perverse interest in a rival agency, much to Evelyn's discomfort. This evening didn't help matters any, for if Jim were irritated with Polly, it is reasonable that he should, man-like, take his irritation out on Polly's friend.

She shook her head worriedly. What a mix-up! That Polly! Somebody ought to shake some sense into the head of the delightfully curved little child who would probably turn out to be the cause of a perfectly good account lost forever. . . .

"BUT, JIMMY, DARLING," Polly was saying an hour later, "it's only a game."

Seated before her dressing table she was, he had to admit, charming in a pink and white way. There was a certain air of delicacy about her which used to enchant him, but which now merely irritated him.

The softly frilled robe she was wearing gaped to reveal the round little breasts. They pressed forward like inverted teacups. There was a softness about the white flesh over the rounded shoulders, a warmth to the loveliness of the neckline, a certain delicacy of wrist and ankle and waistline. But the man saw none of it.

"We should have made that score," he growled, yanking off his collar bitterly. "With the cards you held—"

She twisted around to face him. "Oh, Jim, I do so hate post-mortems, and bridge bores me so." She dimpled at him. "Come over here and let me kiss away all that bad temper."

He took her in his arms perfunctorily. As always her closeness acted like magic upon him. "You really ought to be more practical," he told her, rumpling the silken curls, gathering her close to him, possessing those softly curved lips. "Spending all your time at fortune tellers and movies! Aren't you ashamed of yourself? Why don't you spend a little time doing things?"

She sighed deeply as she nestled down in his arms. Jim was so very clever, it was sometimes a great strain keeping up with him, and she loved those funny tea rooms where dark eyed girls read the tea leaves and told one impossibly marvelous tales. It helped her over some of the worrisome details of living with Jim.

"I really will try to be better," she murmured, giving herself over to the softly caressing fingers of the man, trying not to be completely overcome by the breath-taking excitement which his lips, buried in the softness of her flesh invariably set up within her.

Yet the following day Polly found herself worried more than usual. Frank was Evelyn's husband, and she had no business being with him.

"Look," he was saying, "you and I are in the same boat. I have a damned clever wife—you have a brilliant husband. And what does it get us?"

"A lot of worry," the girl mourned.

"And how! Golly, I'm glad I bumped into you on the street. You know, Polly, you're an awfully cute little number!"

His eyes swept over the dark little frock she was wearing, and as he noted the soft flare of the round curves there was a light of appreciation which gleamed in their depths. Under that warmth, the woman fairly twinkled. She nodded, accepting another drink, and sighed once more—this time not so deeply. His arm, around her waist, was comforting.

"What do you say," his lips close to her ear, coaxed. "We—sort of celebrate—finding each other?"

Her eyes were wide with interest.

"What fun," she agreed. "We ought to do something quite—quite—"

"Goofy," he supplied.

She nodded happily, and the agitation which went on beneath the bodice of the gay little frock was no greater than the agitation which stirred him to gather her very close.

Not five blocks away the man and woman seated in the modern office were staring at each other. Evelyn's long legs were stretched out before her, their silken curves forming twin lines of beauty. She contemplated the tips of her slim shoes thoughtfully.

"That's one of the best campaigns you've ever had, Jim," she was saying. But the man was not listening. He sensed rather than saw the bland perfection of her voluptuous figure, and as she rose to saunter across the room, he noted with appreciation the wide flare of the generous hips, the deep loveliness of the breasts, the dramatic black and white of hair and skin. She was a woman built for life—a woman with long, slim thighs and deeply promising eyes.

"You know, Evelyn, there's something remarkably exciting about you," he blurted out. "There's something . . ."

She perched herself on the edge of the desk, one long leg draped over a rounded knee. The position made the tight skirt creep a trifle higher, and where the material was slit a bit, he caught sight of a tiny bit of ecru lace. It trembled for a moment against the warmth of a creamy thigh, and then was lost to sight as she shifted her position.

"Evelyn," his voice was unsteady, but his arms around her were as demanding as his lips crushing against her own. "Evelyn—Evelyn—I'm so darned sick of these fluttery little women . . . I—you know—"

"Shhhh." She held him in a comforting embrace. He could feel the loveliness of her, the nubile curves of those twin hillocks boring against his hungry body. Her lips were warm and sweet. "I understand, darling," she was saying. "Ah, you don't know—how well I understand . . ."

And as his hand reached up to unfasten the jeweled clasp at her neck, her own long white fingers covered the back of his head, as though his kisses were not to be lost—as though the hunger surged through her with the same goading insistency as his sudden discovery of her charms thrilled him.

As ANYBODY KNOWS, a balmy day does things to even sensible people, and Evelyn, looking over some cosmetic copy sighed deeply. It was difficult staying indoors on such a day, but it was doubly difficult knowing that Jim's office, not too far away, sheltered an equally restless worker.

As though her mind brought forth the thing she wanted, the phone at her elbow pealed its strident demand.

"Evelyn," Jim's voice was positively gay. "I have the car right nearby. What do you say we dash off somewhere? Just you and I."

"But—" She could feel the insistence in his voice, and closing her eyes, she seemed to see in her mind's eye, the brightness of his nearness, feel the thrilling closeness of him as though the memory of that last kiss lingered in all its accuracy. "I'd love it," she agreed impulsively. "Although, Frank said something about dropping in at luncheon."

There was a pause. "The country would

be beautiful today. I know of a charming little place," Jim was saying.

Evelyn laughed delightedly. "I'll meet you in fifteen minutes."

He stole a glance at her. The powerful car was being nosed gently through the city traffic. The fleeting landscape, passing by the windows, seemed to have an eerie quality, but it was nothing compared to the beauty of the woman by his side, Jim thought.

Beneath that tiny hat, a single strand of hair escaped to whip across the white cheek. It's blackness seemed darker against that pure background, and the girl laughed at his expression of sheer amazement.

"I always forget that you're so lovely," he gathered her close to him, his lips covering her willing mouth, his hands stroking the swelling curves of her pliant body.

"Jim, be careful. The chauffeur . . ." she protested laughingly.

"Don't be silly. I picked him for his poor eyesight," the man grinned down. "Listen, darling, this little lodge where we're going. . ."

Evelyn had no illusions about Jim, but the man held a fascination for her which Frank completely lacked. There was a ruthless recklessness about Jim which goaded her on far beyond the point where she knew she ought to stop.

She laughed lightly, but there was nothing light in the caress which enveloped her nor was there anything light in the embrace with which she answered.

THEY SANK BACK, SHAKEN for a moment, by the blinding rush of their newly found emotion. The funny little houses, set farther and farther apart now that the country was becoming sparsely populated, seemed to be mere smudges on a rolling landscape.

"Come back in three hours," Jim directed the chauffeur when, at last, they drew up in front of the great mansion which was set in a knoll of trees. "Take the car, of course. You'll find some place along the road to get a bite to eat. Three hours, remember."

"That will get us back to town by six or seven," Evelyn figured, nodding in approval. "Time enough for dinner."

"And early enough to avoid any questions, eh?" Jim grinned at her broadly.

He approved of her slim figure in its trimly cut suit, but more than that he heartily approved of her air as they were ushered into the private dining room which he had taken the care to reserve. There was just a faint mixture of pleasurable surprise with a dash of smiling understanding which tickled him.

Polly, now, would have either gasped or taken it for granted, but then, of what need had he to reserve a room when Polly was with him? He found himself smiling a bit at this foolishness.

"Are you as happy as all that or is that smile merely a diabolical plot to hide your true intentions?"

"I never knew—until today—in the car—" With a gesture he brushed aside her little evasions and came directly to the point of the escapade. "You feel the same way—about us?"

A TINY FROWN MARRED the perfect features of the woman. Evelyn was a woman who did not like to be rushed. There was a certain subtlety about Frank's approach which always delighted her; this blundering insistence on Jim's part struck a discordant note.

"I thought it was plain—the way I felt about—us." She spoke slowly, thoughtfully, and was going to continue, but the man had stretched out his arms, and drawn her into a wild, insistent embrace.

"I had to know," he murmured, his lips crushing against her own, his trembling fingers caressing her, his words, unsteady and torrid. For a moment she sat stunned, overwhelmed by this sudden display, and then, as the arms tightened, as the lips loosened the stiffness of her mouth, she felt herself yield to the thrilling touch of his hands. Almost involuntarily, she found herself drawn close to that pulsating body as a slender rod of steel is drawn to the embrace of a powerful magnet, and even as she was overcome by a force more irresistible than any she had yet encountered, she gloried in the power he had over her.

The late rays of the afternoon sun picked out the design on the rug, when at last those arms were withdrawn, and the girl lifted her dark, tousled head from his shoulder.

"Jim," her lips were unsteady. Held close to his ear, the brushed a light kiss against the lobe. "Ah, Jim—it has been wonderful—wonderful—"

He gave her an understanding hug. "We'll see each other soon again, Evelyn. Just as often as we can get away."

For a moment they remained thus, but it was Evelyn who at last broke the magic of the moment.

"I'd better make some repairs," she laughed

a trifle self-consciously. "After all, I take it your chauffeur is not wholly a fool."

SHE SHRUGGED INTO THE jacket quickly, glancing at Jim through the mirror to see if he had noticed her. Then, seeing his grin, she laughed.

"Where the devil is that fellow?" the man snorted some fifteen minutes later. "I told him to be back by five and it's five-thirty."

They were on the terrace now, but no familiar sedan was in sight.

"Mr. Trent?" one of the waiters approached. "A message for you, sir—came an hour ago, but you left word not to be disturbed." The boy handed him a slip of paper.

Jim read it and cursed softly. "A broken spring!" he announced.

Evelyn's lips made a little circle of dismay. "We'll have to get a taxi— Boy! Here, boy—get a taxi for us—will you. And look up the train schedules."

Waiters were scurrying around, and Jim was in the middle of activity, all of which merely resulted in the rather terrifying discovery that the next train would be not sooner than eight fifty-three—and that the nearest town, some fourteen miles away could not send a taxi before an hour and a half. . . .

"We'll never get back," Evelyn groaned. "Something will have to be done—Frank will be wild—"

"Frank! Hah, what do you suppose Polly will say—or do?"

"Who cares—that little nitwit probably won't know you're gone . . ." Evelyn was so worried that Jim's attitude seemed to her both stupid and boring. Worrying about a woman like Polly, who was a fool anyway. Frank—well, he was dull, but he was no fool, and his anger was something to remember. Evelyn shivered.

"For heaven's sake, *do* something," she cried angrily. "Don't just stand there barking orders!" She stamped in fury, and Jim glared at her. She was, he saw, singularly plain looking, in her rage. Tiny lines jumped into being at the corners of her mouth. There was none of the cuteness about her which possessed Polly when she was in a temper. That brought him back to reality with a jolt. What would Polly say—what would she think!

"Oh, keep quiet," he roared, unexpectedly furious with the hand-wringing tragic act Evelyn was putting on. "Come on, we'll get one of the local farmers to give us a lift."

They got to the station by slow moving

vehicles, and when at last they parted to taxi from the train to their respective homes, both were completely fed up with each other.

Watching her climb in the cab, Jim shook his head in puzzled amazement. There was listlessness about Evelyn, all the devil-may-care attitude having astonishingly disappeared. While she saw in him nothing but a rather stoutish middle-aged man, sincerely worried lest he have a fight with his wife.

SINKING INTO THE FRAGRANCE of her tub, Evelyn sighed deeply. "It's hard to see an illusion go by the boards," she told herself with faint amusement, "but Jim certainly did look like a pop-over that failed to pop. I wonder what Polly is saying at this moment!"

Jim, shrugging into a dressing robe, was glancing at his face critically. "Hope Evelyn isn't having a time with Frank," he murmured, removing the last bit of tell-tale lipstick. "Funny thing about women . . . always squawking about something. Well, I'm glad Frank has her—not for me—" He grinned a little slyly to know what a perfect wife Polly was.

BUT IT WAS REALLY the chauffeur who held the answer to both these questions. Because at the moment, Polly was handing him a neatly folded bill, "It's so lucky you came across us," she was saying, and she had a way of smiling up at him. "It would have been dreadful to be stuck way out in the country that way."

The chauffeur turned away then, because the man by her side was beginning to look impatient.

He murmured quickly, "Darling—we'll make it soon eh? And the next time we'll make sure the car is in working order. Golly, if your car hadn't come along—just when we were changing that tire—"

Polly stood on tiptoes, but she really didn't have to, because he was so willing to sweep down and catch her in his arms. "When," he demanded happily, "can you get away?"

"Oh, any time," she told him gayly. "You know Jim."

He nodded. "And you know Evelyn. Tomorrow?"

She nodded in agreement. And the chauffeur made a mental note to tell his wife she could order that new hat after all. It looked as though it were going to be a lucrative season.

Big Boy Blue

(*Continued from page* 47)

the downstairs door when I left you before, but I didn't go. I thought I saw a figure on the roof and thought I'd better stick around."

"But—he—"

"I turned him over to Clancy a couple of minutes ago and by this time he's at Headquarters. It was Barney, all right. I'd know his mush anywhere."

Bill's face was so close to hers his breath touched her cheeks. Once more the inner rapturous quiver filled Jan. She half shut her brown eyes, parting her vivid lips as she smiled.

"Oh, Bill—"

Then his arms were around her and she was close to him. The subtle feel of the warmth of her body whipped him to quick ecstasy. His kisses were like liquid-fire that burned to Jan's heart. She could only cling to him in a swoon of joy while she felt his hands tremble caressingly, tenderly upon her.

"I gues it was love at first sight, honey! I want to marry you—before I go on duty tomorrow! I—"

"You want to marry a society gal?" Jan whispered.

He laughed happily. "Nuts to that stuff! You can tell me all about it later, but I'll tell you this now. Look, two weeks before she sailed, I gave Sandra Athling a ticket for speeding and if *she* can come within a mile of *your* looks and charm I'll eat the car she drove that day!"

Look Before You Love

(*Continued from page* 20)

listen, Connie, there's something I want to tell you."

Connie's lips thinned. "There's plenty I want to tell you! You insulted me! You insinuated that—"

"Now, wait a minute. I said what I did for a purpose. I just wanted to know whether—"

"Whether I kissed every man I met!"

"No, that's not it. You see, your father told me—"

Connie's eyes became saucer-wide. "My father?" she cried.

He grinned sheepishly. "I suppose I might as well tell you. My name isn't Dick Templar at all. It's Gordon Grange. I've been hearing about you ever since I was ten years old and when I came East and got a job in your father's office I knew everything was all fixed for us to—to—well—to hook up."

"And you didn't like the idea, did you? Well, I didn't either!"

He blushed. "Well, it was sort of like taking a pig in a poke, so when your father told me you were coming in on this train, I decided to get a look at you before—"

Connie's eyes shot sparks. "Before *what?*"

"Before I—I was forced into anything."

Connie leaped to her feet. "Well, you won't be forced into a thing, Mr. Grange. As far as I'm concerned—"

Gordon swept her into his arms. "You love me. Isn't that true?"

Connie fought to free herself. "No!"

"You do!"

"No!"

The train stopped with a jerk and Gordon's mouth came smack up against Connie's lips. So did their bodies. It knocked the breath out of Connie and left her limp in his arms.

A trainman swinging a red lantern hove into view. "Hey!" he yelled. "We're unhooking this car!"

"Not until I get the proper answer," Gordon sang out.

Connie rested her cheek on his chest. "Yes," she whispered.

The trainman scratched his head. He couldn't understand it. Can anybody understand love?

Here's How!

(*Continued from page* 52)

suddenly she was a little frightened. She had never known a man as strong as Percy. She was positive even a little more pressure would break her in two.

And then she found out that was wrong.

That little extra added pressure, judiciously applied in the correct places, made her not care whether she was broken into bits or not.

Her arms lost their strength, dropped to her sides. The skirt was pulled away and she resented even that momentary releasing of Percy's grip. Now she held her own lips up, eager for the kiss.

Sirens started screaming in the street outside. Percy tore himself away and swore. The pawnbroker burst in.

"The bulls," he said needlessly.

"Stall 'em," Percy snapped. "We'll go out the back way." He started pulling Betty along again.

"Wait a minute," she gasped. "My clothes!"

"I got 'em. You can slip into them in the alley!"

And a few seconds later, Betty Anson, daughter of a millionaire, was pulling on clothes she hoped had been fumigated, in a dressing room made of shadows and bounded by ash cans.

"Hurry up," Percy snapped. "Let's get out of here! Moe'll stall the cops, but they got the car now. We'll cut over to the main stem and grab a cab!"

Betty was completely out of breath when they finally got into the cab. Her heart was pounding so she barely heard Percy give some address on the waterfront.

"Cigarette, Babe?" Percy asked when the cab was under way.

"T-thanks," she managed.

"Still sure you can trust me?" Percy grinned.

"No. You're just as bad as the rest of the men," Betty said and she realized her tone was not at all convincing, so she added, "that is unless you kiss me again."

So Percy made her furious by saying, "Better wait a while, Babe. Or we might not get to the party."

Her lips trembled but somehow she kept from telling him she didn't want to go to any other party!

The cab stopped in a forbidding street, made quite aromatic by the back wash of the waterfront. Percy paid the cab and led her down another dark passage while Betty tried to count how many similar passages she'd been in that night.

Then Percy broke open a warehouse door, an empty warehouse, and they went through that. Then came another passage ending this time in a metal door. Percy pounded. When it opened he pushed something white like an envelope inside. Another moment and Betty was whisked through. Another short hallway and then—Betty let out a little gasp.

She knew where she was now all right, for the first time in hours it seemed. She was in the main ballroom of the Yacht Club—and the costume party was in full swing.

"Meet some of the friends, Babe," Percy said.

And then Betty was recognized. A veritable swarm of people washed toward them, all babbling at the same time about her "kidnaping" and how did she escape.

Stan pushed through. "That's him!" he yelled, "that's the kidnaper!"

And everybody laughed. Betty's head was going around so fast she could barely make out voices saying, "Don't be a fool, Stan, that's *the* Doctor Percival Hopkins Adams, you know, the one who's done such excellent work in the slums here! Horribly wealthy, but works hard! And do the people down there love him! He knows more about them than they do themselves. And they'd do anything for him."

Betty realized she'd had examples of that. She heard Percy explaining laughingly that Betty'd been with him all the time, driving. No, they hadn't heard anything about any kidnaping.

Then the police and Betty's father romped in, were satisfied and romped out again.

Percy said, "May I have this dance? After all we might as well put our costumes to use!"

Betty held up her arms, let him crush her to him. But she didn't move.

"S'matter?" Percy asked.

"You're the doctor. You ought to know."

"You diagnose it. I might get it wrong."

"I—Im waiting for that kiss you promised!" Betty reminded.

Percy started to bend over. He stopped and said suddenly, "Not here! I'm not figuring on anything stopping this one."

He started leading her away. "Oh, Doctor," Betty said, "I think the remedy's going to be exactly right—for what ails me!"

Blonde Trouble

(*Continued from page* 14)

letters in your bureau. I know you're only saving lives here during vacation until—"

Val fondled her fervently.

"What else do you know?"

"That you've got to marry me before the twenty-sixth of the month! If you don't I'll lose a trust fund I'm to inherit! That's why I've been chasing you, trying to get this minute to happen and—"

"Well, it's happening!" he said happily, drawing her closer and still closer to his throbbing heart.

. . . Try, Try Again!

(*Continued from page* 9)

her mother's friends and blushed at the right moment. But inside her heart was thudding, "What the hell is John Smith No. 2 doing? Where is Daisy?"

Marjorie was worried almost out of her mind. Daisy *had* set her two eyes on John Smith No. 2. She had reached down in her feminine bag of tricks and had produced each in its turn on him. The last Marjorie had seen of them before she had to hurry off to her room to dress was Daisy asking John Smith No. 2 to dance. That meant that Daisy was going to cling and when Daisy clung that was *something!*

Suddenly Marjorie saw Daisy come sweeping into the drawing room. She was pulling along with her the real John Smith who was the tall, pale, sickly young man of the station platform. She was saying, "Marjorie, isn't it wonderful. John and I are going to be married right after your debut."

And then she saw Daisy turn her head a little and there was John Smith No. 2 in the door . . . not looking at Daisy . . . but looking straight at her, Marjorie. Marjorie saw Daisy's nose go up on a tilt, saw her mouth tighten and the muscles of her jaw work a little. She knew then, with her heart pounding, that Daisy had tried and Daisy had failed!

She stood there then smiling sweetly on her mother's guests, saying the right things at the right time. But she was remembering a breathless moment when she had clung to John Smith's strong young body, when his lips had devoured hers and her own had been warm and responsive. She let her gaze wander over to where John was standing. He was making a motion with his thumb that when all this nonsense was over he'd be waiting in his car. He'd be waiting—*and how!"*

Marjorie let her gaze wander over to where Daisy was hanging on to the tall, sickish real John Smith. She began to snicker. It was hard to snicker and keep her full breasts from jiggling around under the tight white satin. And debs weren't even supposed to have jiggly bosoms! But it had occurred to her, as she buried her nose for a delicious instant in her bouquet, that the joke was decidedly on Daisy after all. They both had John Smiths . . . but oh, good gosh! what a difference there was in those Johns!

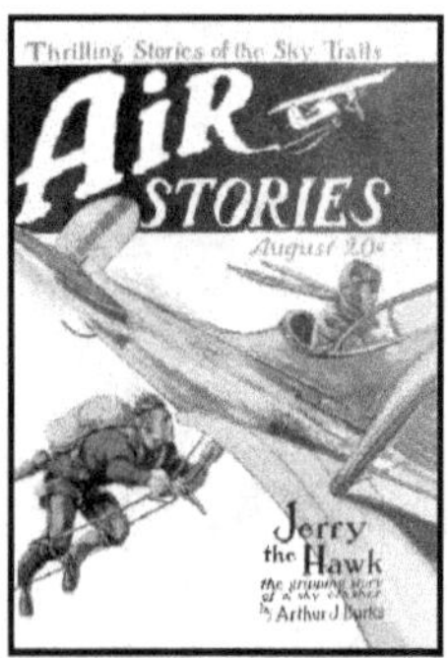

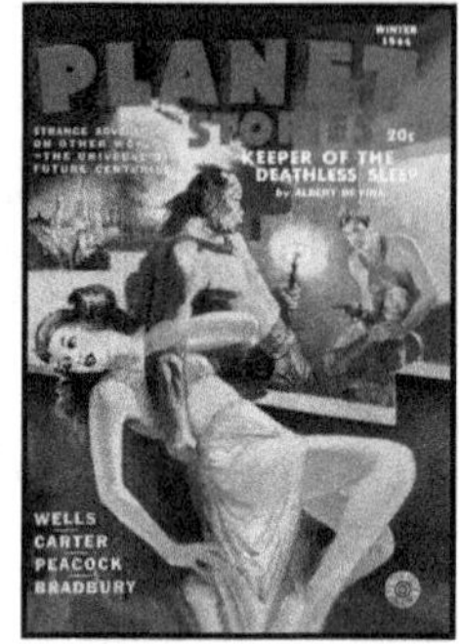

The Fiction House Press Replica Line is available at
www.FictionHousePress.com

Be sure to check our website regularly as we are constantly adding more pulp and digest replicas to our lineup.